SNOW VALLEY CONFESSIONS

MJ MANGO

Copyright © 2025 by MJ Mango

All rights reserved.

No part of this book may be reproduced in any form or by any electronic or mechanical means, including information storage and retrieval systems, without written permission from the author, except for the use of brief quotations in a book review.

ISBN- 9798306723051

Cover design by: MJ Mango

❀ Created with Vellum

For my MP...I miss you like crazy.
So much so that I decided to release a little messy book on your special day.
Happy Birthday.
I love you always!!!

CONTENTS

Chapter 1	1
Chapter 2	5
Chapter 3	8
Chapter 4	13
Chapter 5	16
Chapter 6	21
Chapter 7	25
Chapter 8	28
Chapter 9	32
Chapter 10	35
Chapter 11	39
Chapter 12	42
Chapter 13	45
Chapter 14	48
Chapter 15	52
Chapter 16	56
Chapter 17	59
Chapter 18	63
Chapter 19	67
Chapter 20	70
Chapter 21	73
Chapter 22	76
Chapter 23	79
Chapter 24	82
Chapter 25	85
Chapter 26	89
Chapter 27	92
Chapter 28	95
Chapter 29	101
Chapter 30	107
Chapter 31	110

Chapter 32	113
Epilogue	116
Afterword	119
Acknowledgments	121

1

Maya

"Girl, why aren't you excited?" My friend Terra squealed. I guessed in her eyes I should be excited, but I wasn't. I was nervous because my best friend decided that we had to cash in on a pact that we had made when we were fifteen.

"I wouldn't call it excitement. I honestly can't believe that Jonathan is holding me to this stupid thing. We were two nerdy kids who, if I'm being honest, were in desperate need of a glow-up. No one wanted to date us and so we made the pact."

I remembered it like it was yesterday. Both of us promised that if we weren't married by thirty, we would marry each other and raise a family. We took things way too far for a couple of kids. We even duped our parents into signing it and then we got Jonathan's cousin to be our witness. God, we were stupid.

We hadn't spoken about that crazy idea in years, and all of a sudden, after my thirtieth birthday, I started receiving wedding samples. I honestly thought it was some kind of mistake. I hadn't spoken to Jonathan other than when he called to wish me a happy birthday and promised we would get together soon.

Then came the call from him asking me if I had received them. "Yes. I did, but what are they for?" I asked him confusedly.

"For our wedding. Remember, if we're not married by thirty, we have to marry each other." I'm pretty sure the whole neighborhood heard me gasp.

"Jonathan, you cannot be serious about this. We were just kids."

"Not only am I serious about it, Maya, I will have my firm send you a notice if you don't show up. I still have the paper with your signature on it. Not to mention the fact that we had a witness, and it stated that if either of us broke the agreement, you have to pay the other one million dollars. Do you have a million dollars, Maya?"

"What? Jonathan," I groaned, but it was pointless. Jonathan just kept on talking before he ended the call a moment later after telling me that he would speak to me later about my travel plans.

It wasn't like Jonathan to be so demanding with me. It was strange, but just as I knew my best friend, I knew that he was one hundred percent serious about this. I didn't want to find out what would happen if I didn't show up. I was also a bit curious as to why all of a sudden he was hellbent on us enforcing that stupid contract.

I knew one thing: I couldn't lose him as a friend. Jonathan had been my lifeline as a kid. Growing up, it was just my brother and me, but we weren't extremely close.

Mainly because we were total opposites. I was the nerdy kid, and he was the jock. He excelled in everything sports related, while I only had my schoolwork and projects to get me by.

Jonathan was right there with me. He was my closest friend, and that never changed. Our relationship had been the same for years...until now.

"Girl, get out of your head."

"What? Sorry, Terra. I wasn't trying to ignore you."

"Sure. I don't blame you. My head would be cloudy too if I was about to marry a successful lawyer with everything going for him, including his looks. I mean, I would be excited, not nervous and upset, though."

"That's because you haven't been friends with him for your whole life, and you don't know him as well as I do. He knows every single embarrassing thing about me, and for the main issue, he doesn't have any romantic feelings for me. He never has, and now he's holding me to this pact. So you would want a loveless marriage?"

"It's not loveless. You love your best friend."

"Ugh. Of course, I do, but you know what I mean...And to make matters worse, he's summoning me two weeks early, so I'm leaving tonight. And is my husband-to-be coming to get me? No. He's sending a driver."

My phone notified me that I had a message. I peeped at my phone and saw that I had a message from none other than my best friend. I couldn't help but gasp when I read it.

Kai will be there to pick you up in an hour. Make sure you're ready and dress warm.

Of course, he would send Kai. *Jesus.* Don't get me wrong, Kai wasn't a bad person. He has actually helped me a lot over the years, but of course, it was because of instructions from Jonathan, and he always seemed to be annoyed as if I was a nuisance to him.

I imagined that I probably was. He was Jonathan's other best friend, and well, if he didn't look at me like my presence exhausted him I would probably have tried to fuck his brains out.

The man was...beautiful in all honesty. I knew people said men weren't beautiful, but this man was. I'm talking six-foot-two, thick, muscular build, skin smooth as a baby, and the color of hot chocolate...Mmm.

And I knew that some people hated the food comparison when it came to skin color, but there was no other way to describe this man's perfection. When I looked at him, it has always been the first thing that came to my mind.

His hair was always fresh, as if the barber followed him around daily, and his beard...God, his beard. Every time I saw him I had to keep myself from reaching up and rubbing it.

His smile was like looking at a perfect morning sun. His hazel eyes were so easy to get lost in, his lips looked soft, and every time he licked them I wanted to do the same.

The man walked like he didn't have a care in the world and the way he dressed...I didn't think I have ever seen him dressed down or looking bad. He always looked like perfection, but none of that mattered because Kai didn't like me, and I was marrying our best friend.

"Maya. Girl, where did you go just then?" Terra asked, bringing me out of my thoughts.

"Kai is picking me up."

"Oh. Oh. This is going to be so good."

2

Kai

"What do you want now?" I groaned as I answered the phone for my best friend, Jonathan. He really could be a pain in my ass sometimes. The amount of times he called in a favor from me was disturbing.

"That's no way to answer the phone."

"It is when you call me at seven in the morning because it can only mean one thing. You want me to do something."

"Mmm. Well, at least I don't have to butter you up about it now. Thanks for knowing me so well," he chuckled.

"Yeah. Whatever, asshole. What do you need?"

"Well, for starters…I'm getting married." What the hell?

"What? Congratulations, but to who? Last time I checked you weren't dating anyone seriously." He was a male whore, if I'm being honest. My guy went from a dorky nerd that nobody wanted to snagging any woman he wanted, anytime he wanted, and he used it to his advantage.

"Maya."

"Say that again. I don't think I heard you properly," I said because he couldn't be referring to Maya Gibson. The same Maya that I've known since I was sixteen and met Jonathan...The same Maya Gibson that I was secretly in love with.

Jonathan's laugh brought me from my thoughts. "You heard me right. I'm marrying Maya."

"Why?"

"What do you mean why? Because she's amazing, and we will make a wonderful couple and raise a damn good family together."

"Bullshit." Maya and *I* would raise a damn good family together.

"I'm serious. We're getting married."

"And I was serious when I asked you why."

He sighed as if I was the problem. "When we were fifteen, we made a pact. If we weren't married by thirty, we would get married. She's already thirty and I will be in a week. It's time."

"Are you serious right now?"

"Why wouldn't I be?"

"You would seriously hold her to something that was written when you were fifteen, making her settle? What if she's not happy with that?"

"Doesn't matter. She agreed. We're getting married in two weeks. As my best man, I'm asking you to pick up my bride and drive her to me."

"Jonathan, what's up with you? You care about Maya. I know that much, but right now, you don't sound like it."

"I'm marrying her, aren't I?" He said matter-of-factly, and

for the first time in my life, I wanted to beat my best friend's ass. "Look, if you can't do it, then I will ask someone else or *hire* someone."

"No." I groaned harshly. No way was I going to do that to her. There was no telling how she was feeling. "I will bring her."

"Cool. Thanks, man. You'll need to be on the road by noon if you want to be here by eight. Please be there to pick her up by then and drive safely. You're carrying my precious cargo."

With a grunt, I ended the call. I was pissed at whatever the fuck this was. I couldn't believe it. Maya was going to marry Jonathan. Was this some kind of bullshit game? He couldn't really be serious about this, right?

Had I ever asked Maya out? No, but not because I didn't want to. She just always seemed like my presence was a nuisance to her. I didn't know if she would even go for a man like me.

She was soft and sweet, or at least she was to other people. When she didn't know that I was looking, I always saw her smiling and speaking to people, and when she saw me, it faded.

So, no. I never asked her out, but now I wished I had taken a chance on her, anyway. Maybe she would have said no, but it was too late to try now. She was marrying my best friend. Well, our best friend, but the point was...she was marrying a man that wasn't me.

3

Maya

AT EXACTLY ELEVEN-THIRTY, a knock sounded at the door. I peeped out the window to see a black Range Rover parked on the curve. Kai's black Range Rover. Taking a deep breath, I walked toward the door.

Well, here goes nothing.

"Hi, Kai," I said as I opened the door. He looked me up and down before his eyes landed on my face.

"Hey. Are you ready?" Short and right to the point...as always.

"Umm...Yeah. I...Just let me grab my bags." I turned away from him and walked toward my bags. Just as I was about to bend over to grab them, he moved around me.

"Got it."

"Oh. Thanks." I watched him roll my oversized suitcase

in one hand, grab the two duffle bags ,and head out the door.

"God, that man is fine," Terra said from behind me. "Anyway, here. This is your bachelorette gift from me. It's lingerie. You know, in case things get spicy before I come up for the wedding."

"Stop. Things are *not* getting spicy. Don't joke like that." I was still hoping that I could talk Jonathan out of this mess.

"Take the gift anyway. Gonna miss you, girl. This place won't be the same without you." We hugged goodbye and then I headed down to the opened front door that waited for me. No sooner than the door closed, did we pull away from the townhouse that Terra and I had called home for so long.

Silence.

We rode in complete silence for three of the longest hours of my life. Why couldn't this man just...try to hold a conversation with me?

"Are you cold?" Kai's deep voice broke into my thoughts.

"What?" I turned my head toward him, slightly confused. Not at his question, but more that he had actually said a word to me.

"You keep fidgeting and rubbing your hands together. Are you cold?"

"Umm...A little, yes." More silence. He answered me by turning on the heat and turning back toward the road. After that, he was back to ignoring me.

Since I knew that there was no hope of me having a fun road trip with this man, I decided to lie back and try to sleep. Grabbing my blanket from the back, I spread it out and pulled it over my face.

I willed myself to go to sleep, but of course, it took forever. It seemed like I had just really gotten into my sleep when I felt the car starting to slow down and come to a stop.

Sitting up, I removed the cover and saw that we had stopped at a small gas station just off the highway.

"We're getting gas. It might be a good time to go to the restroom. I don't expect to stop again." Kai said before exiting the car.

He frustrated me. He fucking frustrated the hell out of me. Don't get me wrong, I appreciated every single thing that he had ever done for me, but would it kill him to act like I'm not a pest?

Knowing that we only had maybe three hours to go, I figured I better listen to him. It was cold as shit outside, so I zipped my coat up and headed inside. It didn't help, not one damn bit.

It was cold as shit outside. Hell, I didn't even know where the hell we were. I walked into the gas station, went to the one available bathroom, and ran right into Kai as he was walking out. Ugh. A quick trip in and I was out and heading for some hot chocolate.

"Young lady," the store attendant said. He looked like a nice old man who could be old enough to be my grandfather. "We're closing in about five minutes. I was just telling your fellow that you barely caught us."

I thought that was odd since it was only about five or six in the evening. "Oh. Do you usually close so early?"

"I do when there's a snowstorm coming."

"A what?" Surely, I didn't hear him correctly.

"A snowstorm, ma'am, and seeing as we're in Snow Valley, Wisconsin, I hope you're prepared. According to the news, we're expecting heavy snow for the next few days. I advise you to get off the roads soon."

"Shit...Sorry. Can you stay open just a moment longer while I go talk to him, please?"

"Alright, Miss, but don't take too long. The wife is

already calling to see what time I will be in. Got a pot of chili waiting for me," he chuckled.

I thanked him and walked out to talk with Kai. He was slowly pacing back and forth while he spoke to who I assumed was Jonathan. He looked highly irritated.

"What the fuck do you mean? I asked you when I was on the way to pick her up, and you clearly fucking said you checked everything and the weather should be good until around midnight."

Yep. He was definitely mad. I had never seen him speak to anyone that way.

"We just got into Snow Valley according to the gas station worker...Yeah...Alright but hurry the fuck up. I can't have her out here in this shit."

"Everything okay?" I asked like an idiot. Of course, things weren't okay. We were probably going to be stuck out here in his car on the side of the road, fighting for our lives.

"That...ahh...That was your *fiancé*." Did I imagine him groaning the last word? "Apparently, he knows someone about forty-five minutes from here and they have rentals. Maybe we can get into one for the night. Don't worry about it. Go in the gas station and grab you some snacks and whatever else you need just in case."

He handed me his card, but instead of taking it I grabbed my purse from the car and headed back in. Hmm. What should I get when I have no idea if we will have shelter or not? I also didn't know how long we would be stuck.

I walked around the store and grabbed all of my favorites, especially my chocolate bar with almonds, baked lays, and my precious Dr Pepper. I grabbed a pair of thick gloves and a hat and headed toward the register.

When I got there, I thought about Kai. He hadn't gotten

himself anything, and I could see him back on the phone through the window. He still didn't look too happy.

"Just a moment," I said to the man before turning around and grabbing Kai a few things as well. I came back, paid for them, and thanked the man for staying open a few minutes more. I nervously headed back to the car. Kai was off the phone, but his mood didn't seem to be any better.

"Hey. What did Jonathan say?" I asked as I approached the car.

"He spoke to the guy. He's holding one cabin for us but according to him we need to hurry because the weather is coming fast."

"Okay," I said nervously. We climbed in the car quickly and got on the road. I couldn't stop fidgeting because I was so damn afraid to be in bad weather. If we got stuck, we'd probably die out here. There's no telling how long it would take someone to get to us.

"Hey," Kai said in a tone that I had never heard from him before. It was soft and...comforting. Surprisingly, his hand reached over and covered mine. "You're going to be okay. We will get there in time and let the storm blow over. Relax."

For a moment, I looked at him. I don't know what I was looking for, but he must have known what I needed. He glanced at me and gave me a small smile. I was still afraid, but the touch of his hand and his smile eased my fears just a bit.

The storm was coming fast, and it was unpredictable... but I knew that Kai wouldn't let anything happen to me if he could help it. I knew that he would take care of me. He always has.

4

Kai

FUCKING JONATHAN. I didn't think I had ever been so pissed off in my life. I didn't know what the hell was going through his mind, but I would not put Maya's life in danger because he was being an inconsiderate ass.

Jonathan wasn't usually like that, especially when it came to Maya, but apparently, he had lost his fucking mind and that pissed me off. We should never have been on the road in the first place and not just because she had no business marrying him. It was just after the holidays...Why was he doing this now?

Twenty minutes into the drive to the cabin, the snow started and the further north we drove, the worse the roads were.

"Kai, please slow down," Maya whimpered.

"I can't slow down, Maya. The man whose cabin we're

renting is waiting for us. We'll be there soon, and then we will follow him to the cabin. Just close your eyes, and we should be there in about fifteen minutes or so."

If I could comfort her more, I would. I would hold her hand and give her as much strength as I could. I would wrap her in my arms and hold her tight, but I couldn't. She wasn't mine, and I had to remember that.

When the guy at the gas station mentioned that the storm was coming, I should have checked the weather on the route because the snow was coming down heavily now.

About thirty minutes later, because I did in fact have to slow down, we pulled into the gas station parking lot that the guy was waiting at. "Stay here." I said before exiting the car at the same time he did.

"Hey. You Kai?" he asked.

"I am."

"Good. I'm Randall. You can trail me up. Thankfully, one of the lower cabins was empty. It won't take us but about five minutes."

"Thank you. I appreciate it. Any chance I can catch a store or restaurant open?"

"Don't worry about it. My wife and I had stocked that cabin with all kinds of food since we thought it would be filled. The cabin comes fully stocked, and that includes a grocery order. As long as you can make do with what they ordered, there is no need for the store."

"Damn. That sounds amazing, and I will pay you extra for the groceries."

"No need. Now, let's get you all inside before it gets any worse."

Even though I was pissed at Jonathan, I was thankful for him finding somewhere we could stay for the night. Maya was scared shitless, and we needed to be off the road. The cabin was slightly on a hill but thankfully it had level parking.

"Come on, Maya. Let me help you inside," I said as we exited the car.

Randall let us in and gave us several instructions on things in the cabin. "Anything else you need?"

"No. I think that's it."

"Okay. Your cabin is the only cabin on this end of the road. The trucks will come around and shovel. If you look down and the road to your cabin isn't done, none of them are. Don't try to come down until they are."

"Gotcha. Thanks, man. I appreciate it." I locked the door behind him and turned toward Maya. "The bedroom is that way. Go ahead and relax a bit. I'm going to grab our bags."

"I can help."

"No. I got it. Go relax." I hadn't realized that I growled until I saw her flinch. Shaking my head, I stepped outside and took a deep breath before heading down the steps. It's going to be a long fucking night.

5

Maya

KAI WAS STILL ANGRY. I could feel and see that, but damn...it wasn't my fault that we were in this situation. Hell, I was scared shitless out there. I didn't need his grumpiness on top of it.

Deciding to leave Mister grumpy ass alone like he wanted, I headed to look for my room and realized that there was only one. *Well, this night is going to be interesting.*

I walked into the room and was in awe at how beautiful it was. The room itself was huge. A big king-size bed sat in the middle of the room. A fireplace sat in front of the bed with a tv on the wall above it.

By the window was an all-white rocking chair and a bookcase full of books. On the wall near the door was an oversized chaise that could easily be a bed. I'd decided then that I would be sleeping there.

It had been a long day. I was tired and exhausted. Hell, I was starving too, but I knew that I needed to rest my mind. Grabbing the blanket, I laid down, hoping to just rest my eyes for a few minutes.

I was startled out of my sleep when I felt the cover moving away from me. I was a light sleeper, so it didn't take much. I opened my eyes to see Kai putting the blanket at the foot of the bed.

"What are you doing?" I asked.

"I...was going to put you in the bed." He was going to do what now?

"I'm fine right here. You take the bed since it's only one."

"I'm taking the couch."

"You won't even fit on the couch. I'm small. I can fit anywhere."

"Maya, you're taking the bed, and I'm sleeping on the living room couch. No way in hell am I sleeping in here with you."

"Excuse me. What's wrong with sleeping with me?"

He looked at me like *I* was the problem when clearly he was being an ass, as usual. Without saying a word, he turned around and walked out. This was going to be a long fucking night.

∽

IT WAS WELL into the night when I finally decided to come out of the bedroom. Deciding that it was best to avoid the grump, I settled down in the rocking chair with a book and read to my heart's content. Well, more like until my stomach wouldn't stop fucking growling.

Everything was dark when I walked out, so dark that I had to use my flashlight to get to the kitchen. I quietly tiptoed so I wouldn't wake Kai who was stretched out on the couch.

He looked utterly ridiculous with his legs and feet hanging off the couch. I peeped over the couch, only because I was nosy and couldn't help myself.

He laid there, hugging a pillow to his chest, head turned to the side and his mouth slightly parted. For the first time since I'd known him, he looked like a normal human, and somehow that made him even sexier.

Knowing that it was terrible to think that since I was supposed to be getting married, I shook my head and walked over to the kitchen to find something to eat. I knew I couldn't fix something without waking him up and since he'd been driving, I knew he was tired. Before I could think too much, I noticed my name written on a piece of paper taped to the fridge.

Maya, made you a chicken and bacon pasta salad. Just add salad dressing.

Hmm...I grabbed my salad that looked mouthwatering and added dressing. I grabbed a drink and dropped it in the room before heading back for my bags.

The rest of the night I tried hard to relax but couldn't. The day had been long, and the silent cabin only made my mind wander to Jonathan and the situation that he'd put me in. To make matters worse, I hadn't spoken to him at all since I left. For a man who was supposed to be my fiancé, arranged or otherwise, he didn't seem to be too concerned with me.

Jesus, what was my life turning into? I didn't have a clue if I would be able to convince Jonathan not to marry me and that scared the hell out of me. If I couldn't, my life would never be the same.

Morning came around a little too quickly for me. I

wanted to sleep in a little longer, but my body was so used to getting up, and on top of that, I was a little cold. The thin pajamas that I put on didn't help not one bit, and unfortunately, I didn't have a robe.

Wrapping a blanket around me, I left the room in search of coffee. I passed by the opened bathroom door, entered the living room area, and found that it was empty. The kitchen was also empty.

"Kai?" I yelled without getting a response. "Kai." Nothing. I walked around the entire cabin, which wasn't but a few rooms, and found nothing.

Oh, my God. Did he leave me? Surely, he didn't, but in my panic, I wasn't thinking and ran out the door to check. I didn't see his car. It scared the shit out of me. I was in such a panic that I wasn't paying attention and slipped down the steps.

"*Maya,*" Kai yelled. Where the fuck had he been? I didn't know, but he came over and lifted me from the ground. "What are you doing out here with no clothes and shoes on? Are you trying to get sick?" He groaned as he walked up the steps with me as if I weighed nothing.

"I...I thought you left me." My chest rose and fell as I tried to get control of my breathing.

"Why would you think that?" *Because you don't like me. Because you look at me like being around me is the last thing that you would ever like to do.*

"Kai, put me down."

"Stop struggling." He groaned...again. This man was always groaning and grunting when it came to me, and I was damn well sick of it. He lowered me to the couch, and I immediately tried to get up. "Sit."

"Excuse me?" *Who the hell does he think he is?*

"I said sit. Don't test me, Maya," he said as he walked away.

"Being around your attitude is unhealthy."

"Being around *you* is unhealthy." *Whoa.* I was only joking, even though he couldn't see the smile on my face because his back was turned. He wasn't, though. He was one hundred percent serious because when I looked back toward the kitchen, his face said it all.

I sat there trying to reel in my hurt feelings so he wouldn't notice and he walked back into the living room with a homemade ice pack. "Where does it hurt?" he asked.

"I got it," I groaned, not wanting his help.

"You want to be stubborn?" He dropped the ice pack on the table. "Fine."

6

Kai

I watched as Maya forced herself to stand and limp back to the bedroom. On one hand, I wanted to apologize and help her. On the other hand, I knew I had to stay away from her.

I was being an asshole. I knew that, but I didn't even think I could help it. I was frustrated and angry, but it wasn't her fault and I needed to remember that. Lashing out at her wouldn't do any good.

Don't get me wrong, I was pissed and frustrated at the whole situation, but that wasn't why my emotions were high. When I woke up this morning, I quietly checked on Maya and saw that she was still sleeping.

I figured it would be a good time to see how the roads were. I tried looking at the local news and trucks were making their rounds for the roads. However, more snow was coming, so if we were leaving, we needed to get a head start.

I'd walked a little down the driveway to check the road only to find that it hadn't been cleared yet. I walked back up toward the cabin, deciding to stop at my car that I had moved under the covering last night.

I was only in my car for a moment when I heard Maya call my name in a panic and then I couldn't do anything but watch as she tumbled down the stairs. If I'm being honest, it scared the shit out of me.

I thought she was fucking hurt and tried to take care of her, but she was being stubborn. Hell, it didn't take much for my emotions to get the better of me when it came to Maya, and today was no different.

Now I felt like an ass because I'd fucked around and said some shit that hurt her feelings. I wasn't trying to, but I was being truthful...being around her *was* unhealthy for me.

Jonathan was my best friend and while I didn't understand their engagement, I didn't want to betray him either. I was also still trying to figure out why she was going along with it. I can't see Jonathan forcing the idea, not with her, so why?

Not wanting to bother her and needing something to do, I did what I always did when I needed to relax...I got my ingredients ready to cook. Turning on my light jazz, I got started on some breakfast. We may as well eat a good meal since we were going to be stuck here a little longer.

The whole time that I was cooking, she didn't come out of the room. I hoped that she would so I wouldn't have to awkwardly go into her room to get her after pissing her off.

Since I had no such luck, I plated the food, poured us something to drink, and set everything on the table. I waited a few more minutes, but she still hadn't come out.

I went to her door and knocked, but she didn't answer. I didn't hear anything on the other side and figured she was just still mad at me, so I opened the door and almost dropped to my knees at the sight before me.

Maya had just walked out of the bathroom with a towel wrapped around her, hair wet and pulled to the side. She was fucking breathtaking and I was stunned into place until she realized I was watching.

"What are you doing?" She looked at me like I was some creep.

"Sorry." I cleared my throat. "I knocked, but you didn't answer. Breakfast is ready when you're done." I closed the door and walked back toward the kitchen.

A few minutes later, she came walking out and if I didn't know any better, I would think she was trying to give me a heart attack. She'd put on one of those black long sleeve bodysuits and a long cardigan.

Fuck. She looked good.

"Thank you for breakfast," she mumbled as she sat at the table. I reluctantly joined her but tried my best to ignore the fact that she was there until her fucking moaning started.

"Mmm...Wow. This is really good. I had no idea you knew how to cook."

"I better know how to cook since that's how I make my money."

"Oh. You're a chef?"

"I am." Why didn't it surprise me that she didn't already know that?

"Wow. I never knew that," she said with her eyebrows furrowed.

"That's because you never bothered to ask."

She paused mid-chew and looked at me for a moment before nodding her head with a look that I wasn't sure of. "You're right. I never asked."

It was one of the reasons that I never bothered to approach her. Over the years, she has shown zero interest in me or anything that has to do with me. It didn't matter how many times we've seen each other or how many times I've been there for her, I wasn't who she wanted.

7

Maya

YOU'D THINK I would be embarrassed after walking out with only a towel on and seeing Kai. I'm not, because for the first time, I noticed that Kai looked at me with something other than annoyance on his face.

He looked at me with desire. I don't know if it was just the moment of seeing me half naked or what, but the desire was there. That shouldn't make me happy because I'm technically engaged to Jonathan. I knew that wanting to see that same desire in his eyes was dangerous, but I did. I wanted to see it...I needed to see it.

That's why I dressed in this all-black jumpsuit. I wasn't blind to the way it hugged my body, and let's face it, black was my color. There was something about my brown skin being wrapped in black that was just...sexy.

When I walked out, I watched as his eyes widened. I

watched his throat as he swallowed hard before looking away. On the inside, I was enjoying every second of his eyes being on me, but I knew that it could never go anywhere. Until I got to Jonathan to convince him otherwise, I was marrying Kai's best friend.

As I sat down and ate, I was surprised at just how beautiful and tasty the food was. I wouldn't have guessed that Kai was a chef, but more than anything I was shocked at his response to me.

He was right of course. I had never bothered to ask him about his job. I had never bothered to ask him anything about himself at all, and it made me wonder if maybe he hadn't been the one with the problem after all.

"Maya? You okay?" Kai sounded concerned, and I realized that he must have said something while I was lost in my thoughts.

"Sorry. Did you say something?"

"Yeah. I said the roads haven't been cleared yet. I'm not sure how long it will be before we leave. Are you okay?" He looked at me with his eyebrows furrowed.

"I'm fine. I was just thinking about something…Have you spoken to Jonathan?" He stared at me for a second before shaking his head.

"No, not since yesterday. Haven't you spoken to him?"

"No. Why would you assume I did?"

"Because he's *your* fiancé." He groaned before standing, grabbing his half-full plate, and dropping it on the counter with a bang.

"What's your problem, Kai?"

"I don't have a problem." He stormed off into the bathroom, closing the door behind him.

A smarter woman would let it go because he was pissed

about something but call me what you want...I stood at that door and waited.

I didn't know what he was doing in there, but it damn sure wasn't using the bathroom. After a few minutes, the door opened, he walked out, but stopped in his tracks when he saw me standing there with my arms folded across my chest.

"Do you have a problem with me?" I asked.

"No."

"Are you sure? Because I get the feeling that you do. After your moment of *assholeness* this morning, I started fresh and felt wonderful until a few minutes ago. So, if you're going to ruin my mood, you're going to tell me why."

Silence. He just looked at me like he was looking through me.

"Do you have a problem with me marrying Jonathan?" I got the feeling that he did because every single time that I mentioned Jonathan, he seemed to have an attitude.

"Maybe I do."

"Why? Why is any of it your business, Kai?"

"Don't ask questions that you don't want the answer to," he said as he walked away. "I'm going to see if the roads are clear

8

Kai

THAT WHOLE SPEECH that I gave myself about keeping my feelings in check didn't work, not one damn bit. I thought I was doing pretty good at first. I managed to sit down at the table with her and eat.

Then, she asked me about Jonathan, and it really got under my skin. For a few minutes, I had allowed myself to forget about everything else and enjoy her time. Her mentioning him was like her putting my fire out. I wasn't mad at her. I was mad at myself, but not as mad as I was at the situation and the crazy fucking weather.

The roads still weren't cleared, and it had already started back snowing. I was sure that we would be spending the rest of the day and night here, but the problem was the cabin wasn't big enough for the two of us.

I took my time walking back to the cabin, wanting to

avoid her at all costs and hoping that she would be in the room by the time I made it back in. Of course, I had no such luck. When I stepped through the door, Maya was sitting in the living room. There was a wooden tray on the coffee table with two coffee mugs and some muffins that I saw in the pantry earlier.

She looked at me with a tight smile, and I wasn't sure what the hell was going on. "Can you come and sit?" She asked.

"What's all of this?"

"Coffee. You drink coffee, don't you?"

"I do."

"Good. Have coffee with me."

"Umm."

"It's just coffee, Kai…and conversation. That's all. I'm not going to bite." I slowly made my way to the couch, opting to sit as far away from her as possible. Grabbing the mug, I took my first sip.

"I was wondering if we can't get along because we don't know each other." I shook my head at that.

"We've known each other since we were teenagers."

"Yes, but we don't know each other. All this time and I didn't even know that you were a chef. You're right. I never asked, so I'm fixing that."

"Why?" She confused me. I had just argued with her and walked out. Shouldn't she be just as pissed as she was the first time? She was sitting there acting as if nothing happened.

"It just feels like the right thing to do." She shrugged. "Do you have any siblings?" I couldn't help but laugh at her question. "What's funny?"

"Nothing, Maya. No. I don't have any siblings."

After a moment of silence, she sighed heavily. "Kai, in a

conversation it's polite to ask questions, too. You didn't ask me."

"You have a brother named Miles. Your parents' names are Robert and Brenda, whom I have met before."

"When did you meet my parents?"

"At your graduation."

"You were there?" Of course, she didn't remember that I was there. She was too caught up in spending time with Jonathan before he hit the road. Never mind that I was the one that brought him to the graduation in the first place.

I hummed in response and watched her eyebrows furrowed in confusion. "I spoke to your parents for quite a bit at dinner before heading home."

"Kai, you can't be serious."

"Why is that?"

"Because I would have noticed that you were there."

"You had a lot of family around, some friends, and classmates. It's definitely easy to miss someone." *Especially if they're not even on your radar.*

"I'm sorry."

"For what, exactly?"

"For not noticing, just like I never realized that I never asked you anything about yourself. I was always so quiet around you because I thought you didn't like me. You always seem annoyed with me."

"I am always annoyed with you because you never see—"

"See what?" I shook my head and tried to stand before Maya's hand reached over and pulled me back down. "No. Stay and talk. When you get irritated, you run. We're stuck here together. We may as well talk."

She wasn't lying. I did run off when I was irritated, but mainly because I try to keep my temper in control.

"Kai, you said that you're always annoyed with me because I never see what?"

"Me." She gasped and looked at me like she couldn't believe what I was saying to her. I meant every single word and because I was already in deep shit for revealing half of my truth, I may as well finish. "You never see me, Maya. I've always been there for you. I've always tried to get closer to you and yet, you never saw me. I would come to you at the drop of a dime and even though it was me there, you were so thankful for Jonathan."

"Kai—"

"I get it. You called him, and he would call me, but I didn't always show up for you because he called. I showed up because I cared."

9

Maya

SPEECHLESS. I was absolutely speechless at hearing Kai's confession. My mind went back to this morning when I so clearly saw desire in Kai's eyes. My mind also went back to the many times when he griped and groaned over the years. Hell, even when he griped and groaned on the way up here. It was always when I was going on and on about Jonathan.

Has Kai wanted me all of this time and didn't say anything because he thought that I wanted Jonathan? That was ridiculous. I've only ever seen him as my best friend and nothing more.

"I'm sorry, but if you would have just asked me, I would have told you that I don't see Jonathan like that."

"Then, why are you marrying him, Maya?" He looked me in the eyes and for the first time I felt like I saw Kai. I wasn't sure what to say to that question and the truth was I didn't know how to deal with Kai's confession, so I got up and walked away.

"Now who's running?" I heard him say as I walked away.

I was running, running to my fucking phone to call Terra. As soon as I made it to the room, I closed and locked the door. Hell, I even went into the walk-in closet and closed that door.

The phone rang once, twice, and even a third time before she picked up the Facetime call. "Hey, honey."

"Terra."

"Uh oh. What happened?"

"Kai and I had to get off the road last night, and it's still snowing, so we're sort of stuck here for a little bit."

"Oh, my God. Are you okay?"

"Terra…Terra."

"What, girl? You're freaking me out."

"Kai has been acting like a butthole since we left."

"You said that he's always a butthole. What's new?"

"His reason or the fact that I don't think he's been trying to be a butthole at all, Terra…I think he likes me."

"You think?"

"I'm so serious. He said that he's always annoyed with me because I don't see him. Then he tells me how he's been there for me, and he's been to my graduation and—"

"Of course, he was at your graduation. Did you not know that?"

"No. I didn't. I had no idea."

"Wow. I just thought you weren't interested in Kai because of Jonathan. I had no idea that you were blind."

"Blind?"

"Whenever Kai sees you, he can never take his eyes off of you. He always has a look of longing, like everything he's ever desired is wrapped up in you."

"What?"

"He does, Maya. He always has, but I thought that you had feelings other than besties for Jonathan."

"Eww. No. I've never had any feelings for Jonathan."

"Then why are you marrying him?" I groaned in response because Kai had just asked me that. Both of them knew why I was marrying Jonathan.

"What am I going to do, Terra?" I couldn't avoid Kai. We were both stuck in this one-room cabin. I also couldn't just ignore the conversation that we had earlier, either.

"Seduce him." She said with a straight face.

"Stop talking crazy. I'm being serious."

"So am I. You're better than me. You're marrying Jonathan and don't have any feelings for him. I would seduce Kai in a heartbeat if I were you."

"Bye, Terra. I will text you later."

"Don't do anything I wouldn't do."

"Which isn't much." I laughed as I hung up on her. Calling her was obviously a mistake. I didn't need her putting shit in my head. Until I convinced Jonathan otherwise, I was technically his fiancée.

10

Kai

Maya stayed in her room for hours, and that was fine by me. I was in a terrible mood, anyway. I didn't even try to go back down to check on the roads because the snow was steadily coming.

Needing to pass the time, I first watched a movie, and then I went on to cook dinner. I really wasn't in the mood, so I made a simple Cajun pasta and some toasted bread.

After I sat down and ate, I headed to the bathroom to get ready for bed. It wasn't like I was going anywhere. Then it was back to the couch I went, turning on the tv to find another movie. I knew one thing, if we didn't get out of here, I would lose my mind.

I was about twenty minutes into the movie when I heard Maya's bedroom door open. I heard her when she walked into the room. I heard her when she fixed her food and sat at the table to eat. I heard her when she was cleaning up after she was done. I was hyperaware of every fucking thing that had to do with her.

The room was silent for a few minutes until she opened the fridge, then it was silent again. After that, I forced myself to focus on the movie until she cleared her throat.

"Kai," she said softly. I turned to face her, and she held out a bag.

"What's this?"

"A peace offering. I bought you some things from the store." I had seen the two black bags in the fridge and just assumed that they were for her. I never even checked them.

"Thank you." I sat up and opened the bag, smiling when I saw my favorite orange soda and some peanut M&M's.

"You're always eating and drinking that whenever I have to ride with you."

"It's my favorite. Thanks."

"What are you watching?"

"*NCIS.*"

"Mmm...Must be an episode I missed. Mind if I join you?" *Yes, I mind.* The last thing I wanted to do was hang around her.

"Yeah. Sure," I said as I moved over a bit.

The silence was awkward, and I found myself unable to focus on the show. I also knew that she wasn't watching it either. She was too busy looking in her lap and fidgeting.

After a while, she slowly became more comfortable and relaxed. Soon her body turned slightly toward me. She rested her head on the couch, and I listened as her breathing slowed.

She was falling asleep, and I knew that I should have stopped her and sent her to her bedroom, but I selfishly didn't. I found myself staring at her as she slept, taking comfort in her being there next to me without the petty arguments and misunderstandings.

Eventually, I fell asleep, only realizing it when my eyes opened and I felt her hand on my cheek. I opened my eyes to see her face only inches away from mine. Some time through the night, we moved closer to each other.

Her eyes moved from my lips to my eyes. I knew that I should have moved away, but I didn't. "Maya." My voice sounded husky, even to myself.

"What am I doing, Kai?" Her voice was full of confusion and made me uneasy.

"Don't do anything that you would regret." I knew that if I touched Maya that I should regret it, but I also knew that I wouldn't. She may be marrying my best friend, but she was meant to be mine.

It was hard staying in place, but I wouldn't make the first move. If this was going to happen, it would be because she wanted it to. I sat there, staring into her eyes until finally she leaned closer and barely brushed her lips across mine.

It was all the invitation I needed as I pulled her closer and kissed her deeper. Her lips were just as soft as I imagined. I sucked her bottom lip in as I shifted, pulling her onto my lap to straddle me.

I couldn't believe that this was happening. So many years had gone on and I finally had her in my arms. Feeling her body on mine as my tongue explored her mouth made my dick rock hard.

Slowly, I rocked her back and forth, rubbing her against me. I trailed kisses down her neck, listening to her soft moans.

For one single moment, I wanted to look at her. I wanted to see her face as I rubbed her against my cock. It was a mistake. The moment my eyes landed on her face, she paused.

"Oh, my God. I can't do this." Her voice was full of panic. She climbed off of my lap so fast that she almost fell. I wasn't going to stop her. Just as she wanted to leave, I watched her run away.

11

Maya

WHAT WAS I THINKING? Did I want to see what could happen between me and Kai? Yes, but I needed to talk with Jonathan first. I needed to convince him not to go through with this bullshit wedding because I didn't feel right sleeping with another man until I did. He may have just been my best friend, and I may have thought he was gone absolutely nuts, but still. I didn't like mess and confusion.

It's okay, Maya. You didn't do anything. Right. It was just a kiss...A hot as fuck, mind-blowing kiss, but nothing else happened. I could just call Jonathan in a few hours and maybe talk him out of this mess.

I grabbed my phone from the charger and saw that it was early as shit, barely after six. I also saw that I had a missed call and a text from Jonathan last night. He'd wanted nothing more than to check on me, but it was enough to make me feel guilty.

Knowing that he was up, I called even though I knew that it was early. The phone barely rang once before he answered, and it made me wonder what he could have been doing so early. "Morning. You're up early," he said as he answered the phone.

"Morning. Sorry, I missed your call. I went to bed kind of early." *Right next to your best friend, but you don't need to know that part.*

"I saw that the weather was still bad, and the snow was supposed to continue. I would feel better if you and Kai stayed for the rest of the week at least."

"I don't know if that's such a good idea."

"Of course it is. Your safety is important." Yeah, but I wanted to get there soon so I could talk to him. Delaying the rest of the trip would only give me a few days to do it...but on the other hand, maybe being here would give me time to see if there was more than this sexual spark between Kai and me.

"You're right."

"I'm always right," he chuckled. "Well, I'm about to head to the gym. I will talk to you later."

Okay. So, I get to spend the rest of the week with Kai. I'd run away from him feeling guilty, but now all I felt was excitement.

The thing was, there was a real high chance that I wouldn't convince Jonathan of anything and then I would have to marry him. When Jonathan first mentioned it to me, I was honestly shocked because we hadn't discussed it over the years.

Then, the truth hit me and if I was being honest with myself, dating hadn't worked out for me. So, I thought if I didn't convince Jonathan, maybe it wouldn't be so bad. Jonathan would always love me, even if it was just as a friend. I knew that he would take care of me and both of our families loved each of us.

The problem was, now when I thought about it, the thought of marrying him made me feel like a mismatched puzzle that would never be put together. I knew that if I were to leave this cabin without exploring more with Kai, I would regret it. Either we explored more and it worked, in that case, I would refuse to marry Jonathan and take whatever he throws my way...Or it could have been a disaster in which case, this would have been our little secret.

It might have been wrong, but so was blackmailing your friend into marrying you. I only knew one thing: I didn't want to have regrets.

He was probably pissed at me, and I wouldn't blame him. I left him hanging even though it was the last thing that I wanted to do. Trust me, I wanted nothing more than for him to keep his mouth and hands on me.

I wanted everything that he could offer me, but at the time I felt guilty. I felt like I was betraying Jonathan, not because we were supposed to be getting married, but because of the relationship that he and Kai had. The last thing that I wanted to do was mess up their friendship.

I took a quick shower and then headed back out to find the living room empty again only this time I could hear the shower in the other bathroom running.

Just like last night, I stood by the bathroom and waited for him, but this time for a different reason.

12

Kai

It was like déjà vu when I walked out of the bathroom and saw her standing there. The difference was yesterday when she was there, she was ready to pick a fight. Today, I was not so sure why she was standing here and at the moment, I didn't care to find out.

I brushed right past her and walked toward the kitchen because breakfast wasn't going to fix itself. I pulled ingredients for pancakes and omelets out of the fridge and sat them on the counter.

I pulled out the skillet and grabbed the plug for the griddle. I was just about to plug it up when Maya's hand stopped me. Slowly, I lifted my eyes to her.

"Kai...I know that I stopped you earlier. I know that you're upset, but...umm..."

"But what?"

"If you tried again, I wouldn't stop you."

"What changed?"

"I don't want to regret not going for what I want." She leaned her body closer to mine. "I want you, Kai."

I wanted her too, but it wouldn't be that damn easy for her to play with me. I wasn't in the mood for her games.

"Maybe in another lifetime, Maya. Now, if you will excuse me, I need to cook." Instead of responding, she stormed off to her bedroom and slammed the door.

Maybe I was being an asshole. I didn't doubt it, but again, I was pissed. I had wanted her since forever and this morning I thought that she finally wanted me too. Then she'd run off as if her ass was on fire.

I was so frustrated that I hadn't realized that I was just standing there in the kitchen doing nothing. I wasn't in the mood to cook anymore, so I put the food and skillet back up and opted for a bowl of cereal.

A few minutes into my breakfast, my phone rang with a call from Jonathan. "Hey," I said as I answered the phone, trying to keep my tone level so I wouldn't give away the fact that I was pissed and sexually frustrated with *his* fiancée.

"Hey, brother. I talked with Maya, so I knew that you were awake." So, she spoke with Jonathan and then tried to fuck me afterward? What the fuck is that about?

"Mmm." I hummed because what was I supposed to say?

"You good, man?"

"Yeah. I'm great. It's just early as hell. I want to get an early start so we can get on the road as soon as the roads are clear."

"Actually, I told Maya that I would prefer it if you all stayed for the week."

"And why the hell would you do that?"

"Because it's safer. You know that the snow isn't going to

let up for another two days and then the roads will be crowded. Just stay until the end of the week. I will pay for it."

"I don't need you to pay for it. I would just prefer to get her there as soon as possible."

"Why? Are you two not getting along?"

"We're fine."

"Well, then it's settled. Stay until the end of the week, and I will see you all then. Okay. Talk with you later," he rushed out before hanging up, and I had to wonder if he had lost his mind. I knew that he was acting fucking strange but figured I could just check on him when I arrived at his place.

Now, he wanted me to stay the rest of the week with Maya. I was strong enough to deny her this morning, but I doubted that I could last for five more fucking days, and if I wasn't careful…I would be fucking my best friend's fiancée.

13

Maya

"OH, MY GOD. HELP ME," I groaned as soon as I saw Terra's face on the screen. I damn near ran to my room, closed my door, and locked it. I didn't even give her a chance to say anything when she answered the phone.

"What happened, Maya?" Her voice was full of concern.

"I've made a complete fool of myself. Honestly, it's all your fault for putting stupid ideas into my head."

"What are you talking about? You're not telling me anything."

"After I talked to you, I went back out there and tried to make peace with him. I'd picked up his favorite snack from the gas station but hadn't given it to him yet. I used that as a way to soften him. It was nice even though it was awkward. I have to admit that I felt peaceful being there with him. I ended up falling asleep and this morning when we woke up, I kissed him."

"Shut up. Girl, you did what?"

"I kissed him, Terra. I kissed him, and it was the hottest thing. The man can kiss. I swear, I almost had an orgasm from that alone"

"So, what's the problem? Because I don't see one."

"Terra, we were on the verge of doing more. I was in his lap, and we were kissing. Then, I started feeling really guilty because I hadn't talked to Jonathan and well, I stopped him."

"Let me get this straight...the guy that you've had a mild crush on for years finally breaks and openly shows you interest. You all kiss and you stop him. The same man we were talking about earlier because it can't be another one... Are you crazy?"

"Apparently. That's not the part that's driving me crazy, though. After I stopped him, I came into the room and got my head together. I also talked to Jonathan, and he mentioned that we should stay a little longer to be safe." She did her little messy hum.

"So, I kind of talked myself into seeing if me and Kai could have feelings for each other. I figured that we had some days, and I would rather check it out than have regrets. I went back out there, and he rejected me, Terra. I'm so embarrassed." Which is why I'm whining to her like a teenage girl instead of dealing with my mess like an adult.

"Don't be. I mean, I can see why you are, but don't let it get to you. Men are strange creatures anyway, but Kai is a different subject. He confessed that he's wanted you and then you finally seemed to notice him just to change your mind. I think he's the one that's feeling embarrassed and rejected...and rightfully so."

"Ugh, Terra. This isn't going to work."

"Only because you're going to get in your own way. If you truly want to see if you have a chance with Kai, do it, but you're going to have to clear your head before. It wouldn't be fair to him if you didn't."

I knew that she was right, but my ego was still bruised. I had walked in there and waited for him, thinking that I was sexy, and he wouldn't be able to resist me. Now what?

"What do I need to do, Terra? How do I get him to believe that I really want to go there with him?"

"Honestly, I can't tell you that. You know him way better than I ever did. Think about it and act fast. My only suggestion is to make it sexy. Figure out what drives him wild and run with it." Terra said before we ended the call.

Figure out what drives him wild. That was easy. Me. I'd never seen it before, but over the last few days, it was easier to spot and feel. Kai was definitely crazy about me, and if I needed to drive him wild, I knew exactly how to do it.

14

Kai

SHE WAS TRYING to kill me. That was the only way for me to describe her behavior. I'd stepped outside for a few minutes to clear my mind and thoughts of her. I was only out there for a few minutes when I decided that it was too fucking cold to be outside just to avoid Maya.

As soon as I walked back into the cabin, I could hear the shower running, which I thought was odd because she had been showering in her room.

Still needing to clear my head, I walked into the dining room to pour myself a drink when I looked up and could see the bathroom door wide open. There in my shower was Maya. The shower door was closed, but the silhouette of her body was very visible.

Shit. That was the last thing I needed to see since I'd been imagining her naked and under me since we got here.

I poured myself a drink and went to the living room. A few minutes later, the shower stopped, and I heard the shower door. For a little while, I didn't hear anything and figured that she was getting dressed.

So, when she walked out of the bathroom and I turned my head, the last thing that I expected to see was her wrapped in a towel. She paused and looked at me with a smirk on her beautiful face.

"Kai, you didn't mind me using your shower, did you?" She was playing games with me, and if she wasn't careful, I would make her regret it.

"No, Maya," I said before turning my head toward the tv. It was a logical thing to do. To pretend like I wasn't interested, and that I was watching a show. Only she had fried my damn brain and I hadn't realized that the tv wasn't on until I heard her laugh.

"Your *show* looks interesting." She laughed as she walked away. Damn her.

This morning, I had been ready to have her in every way possible until she denied me. She'd walked away from our conversation before and then she'd walked away from me. I had decided that I would stay away from her, but I knew now that it wouldn't be that easy.

"Kai," Maya called for me a little while later. "Can you help me for a second?" I ignored her. Going into her room was a terrible idea, and I wasn't about to do it until I heard a crash coming from the room.

I jumped to my feet and ran into the room to see what was going on. Maya was bent over trying to lift the bookcase that had fallen. "I got it," I said as I stopped her from lifting it.

"Thank you." She stood up to reveal herself. She had on

a very short silky robe and whatever she had on under the robe had her breasts damn near bursting out of it.

I set the bookcase in its place and put the books back on the shelf. "Just stop. I've got it," I said when Maya bent over to help me.

"Fine." She popped her lips like I had said something wrong when I knew damn well I hadn't. Once I was done with the books, I reluctantly stood up. "Thank you."

"What are you wearing?" I couldn't help myself not to ask.

"Umm...My pajamas. They're all I have."

"I find that hard to believe...or maybe not. You were supposed to be with your fiancé after all."

"Why do you keep doing that?" she snapped.

"Doing what?"

"Bringing that up. I've told you that I do not want Jonathan in that way."

"And yet you're still engaged to him."

"You're being an ass." I couldn't argue with that, so I didn't. I was an asshole. I could admit that. I turned to leave, and she grabbed my hand, pulling me back to her. "Where are you going?"

"Out of here before I do something that—"

"Something that what? Something that you will regret?"

"No. Something that *you* would regret." With her other hand, she untied her robe and revealed her black lace panty and bra set. I sucked in air, trying to control myself, but my dick was already rock hard.

She lifted her hand to my face. "I won't regret it."

"Maya." Her name was a plea from my lips because I was hanging on by a thread, and I needed her to stop this shit.

"Kai."

"What are you doing, Maya? Are you trying to make me fuck you?"

"Yes."

15

Maya

Kai's resistance to me snapped like a twig. In an instant, his hands were on me and driving me back toward the bed, pushing me down when the back of my legs hit it.

"You've been teasing me over and over, Maya. Be very careful with what you want. If you want this to stop, tell me now."

"I want you to fuck me, Kai. That is what I want." I was done being the person who over thought every single detail. I was throwing caution to the wind and finally doing something that I've fantasized about for years...having Kai.

His lips came down on mine...hard. Our tongues were in a battle, and he was no doubt winning. His hand trailed down my sides and around to my core. He groaned before grabbing my panties and pulling them with force.

Gasping, I looked at him with wide eyes. "My patience

with you has worn out, Maya. This morning, you could have gotten the nice me, but now...now I'm going to fuck the shit out of you."

"Mmm," I moaned as one of his fingers slid into me. I couldn't believe it. He was actually touching me. So many times I had imagined this, and it was finally happening.

"Fuck. You're so wet." He kissed down my neck before moving down toward my breasts, stopping to unhook my bra and pulling a nipple into his mouth, but only for a second.

Then he continued kissing down, slowly. He kissed my stomach. He kissed my thighs, and finally, he kissed me right where I wanted him to. The feeling of his lips and tongue as it circled my clit had me coming in only a few minutes.

My body trembled as my lips parted. The orgasm overtook me, and I found myself whispering Kai's name. He moaned as if the taste of my cum brought him pleasure. He continued his assault on my pussy until my legs stopped shaking and I relaxed. Then, he stood up and removed his clothes, and my mouth literally watered. Kai with clothes on was sexy as hell, but his body was a work of art.

He had muscles, but his body was thick, not lean. His chest was bare, but his lower stomach had a trail of hair that I found sexy as hell and made me want to trace it with my tongue. Then there was his thick and long dick that I wanted to fill my mouth with.

"Be right back," he said before leaving and coming back with condoms. "They were in the medicine cabin."

"Come here. I want to taste you, too." My mouth literally watered at the thought of him being in my mouth.

"Later. Right now, I need to be inside of you." He rolled

the condom on and climbed back into bed. Okay. We're really doing this.

He climbed between my legs and kissed me again as he rubbed his tip against my entrance. He paused and looked into my eyes. I could see the question in them. *Are you sure?*

"Yes, Kai. I want you."

The words were barely out of my mouth when he pushed inside of me, taking my breath away. "Fuck...Maya." He moaned as he moved in and out of me. "I want to take you. I want to be rough and fuck you like I've always dreamed. I want to punish you for that shit earlier, but I'm not. Now that I have you, I'm going to take my time with you."

And he did. He took his time bringing me to the edge over and over but holding back every time that I was close. I held him close to me, enjoying the feeling of his body on top of mine. I wanted to memorize every feeling, every touch of his skin, and every thrust. I wanted to memorize *him*.

When we'd both had enough of holding it out, he brought me to another orgasm before following me with his. The sound of my name on his lips as he emptied his cum inside of me made me feel like I was floating on top of the world.

He climbed off of me and pulled me onto my side and into his arms. I lifted my head to look at him. I wasn't sure what us having sex meant. All I knew was at the moment, the only thing that I wanted was to stay right there in his arms.

We laid there for a little while longer, neither of us saying a word. I didn't know why he wasn't talking, but I was scared to break the fog. I got what I wanted. I wanted to sleep with Kai, but was that really all I wanted?

Did I want that one time to be it? I wasn't sure, but just as the thought crossed my mind, my phone rang. I leaned over to check who was calling and was surprised to see that it was Jonathan.

16

Kai

BEING with Maya was nothing like I had expected it to be. I'd always pictured us going crazy at each other out of anger, but when I finally had her in my arms, I knew that I needed to take my time with her.

The feeling of sliding into her was like nothing I'd felt before. It felt like I was right where I needed to be. The way that she responded to me made me feel like her feelings were just as strong as mine.

Afterward, I couldn't stop myself from pulling her into my arms. I didn't want to let her go. I wanted to hold her and feel her body on mine forever. I knew then that having her one time would never have been enough.

Then her phone rang, and she gasped when she saw that it was Jonathan. It was like a bucket of cold water being thrown in my face, reminding me that Maya wasn't really mine. It reminded me that I had overstepped, once again, when it came to her, but I didn't regret it. I couldn't even though I should have.

She may not be marrying Jonathan out of love, but she was still technically engaged to the man. And he wasn't some random guy. He was my best friend and while that should make me feel guilty, I knew that if I could, I would make love to Maya over and over again.

She placed her finger over her lips, asking me to be quiet with a pleading look in her eyes. "Jonathan, hi," she said as she answered the phone.

"Hey. Why can't I see you?"

"I...I just got out of the shower. I'm getting dressed."

"Oh." They were both silent for a moment until he spoke again. "You texted me earlier and said that you wanted to talk to me about something. Figured it would be a good time to call since I just got home. What did you need to talk with me about?"

Maya looked at me and swallowed nervously before responding to Jonathan. "Umm...Give me a few minutes and I will call you right back. Like three minutes. I need to finish getting dressed."

"Okay. I'll be waiting." They ended the call and then she turned toward me. I didn't need her to say it for me to know that she wanted me to leave. I climbed out of her bed, grabbed my clothes off the floor, and headed toward the door.

"Kai." Her voice was soft, nothing like the woman who had practically seduced me into sleeping with her. It was like she was two different women.

"Yeah?" I paused at the door and turned toward her.

"I just need to talk with him for a moment. We can talk after, okay?"

"Sure," I said before walking out even though I didn't plan on talking to her at all. She'd spoken to him this morning before coming out there and trying to fuck me. Now she'd fucked me and needed to speak with him.

What's so important that the conversation couldn't wait? She could have easily sent him to voicemail. She gave me hell, but for some reason with him, she was soft-spoken and sweet. He got all of her best…her smiles and warmth, her well wishes and good grace. I got shit.

I was so fucking frustrated that I didn't even bother getting dressed. I laid my covers out on the couch and decided to take a nap. There wasn't any point in me worrying about Maya and Jonathan. Truth was she was his, and I thought that was something that I would have to learn to live with.

17

Maya

KAI TRIED to look neutral when I asked him to give me time to speak with Jonathan, but I could see the look on his face...he was pissed off. Now I was irritated because I've learned that a pissed-off Kai wasn't fun to be around.

I didn't want privacy for any reason other than to speak with Jonathan about the engagement. I'd thought it over since I'd been here, and I'd realized that all this time that I thought Kai didn't like me, he felt the same as I did.

I didn't know. I just felt like we were possibly going to miss out on something that could be great. So, I sent Jonathan a message letting him know that I needed to speak with him and that it was urgent. I just didn't feel right exploring this thing with Kai while I was technically still supposed to marry Jonathan.

It was a conversation that we definitely needed to have,

but Jonathan's call was just bad timing, and I was torn on whether I should explain myself to Kai or speak with Jonathan.

I took a moment to think about it and knew that the conversation between Jonathan and me needed to happen now. Kai was an adult. He could be patient and wait instead of being bull-headed and stubborn, as usual.

I took a deep breath and dialed Jonathan's number. It took a couple of rings for him to answer, and I was starting to think that he wasn't going to until his face came over the screen.

"Did you forget that I was calling?"

"No. I didn't. I was drying my hands, if that's okay with you."

"Oh." I grew silent, not knowing how I wanted to start the conversation.

"What did you want to talk about, Maya?" Really, Jonathan.

"I'm sure that you know what I want to talk about." How could he not?

"I'm not a mind reader."

"Our pending wedding."

"What about it?" I was gonna have to remind myself to kick my dear best friend's ass when I saw him.

"We can't get married."

"Why? Is there a certain reason why you don't want to?" *Yeah. I'm fucking your best friend.* If I'm being honest, that's not all I want with Kai. Now that he's confessed how he's felt, I want so badly to explore the possibility of more with him.

"No. It just can't happen. I'm asking you to drop it, please."

"Can't do that, Maya. It's time."

"Time for you to hold me to something that happened fifteen years ago. Come on, Jonathan, don't do this to me."

"I'm doing what's best for you." Is he serious right now? How the hell could marrying him be what's best for me? Has Jonathan completely lost his mind?

"What's best for me? What makes you think forcing me to get married by threatening to sue me is what's best for me?"

"You don't understand now, but one day you will realize that I was right."

"Jonathan, as my best friend, you've always vowed to do things with my best interest at heart. Now, all of a sudden, you send me wedding ideas and then summon me to marry you. You're using your damn law degree, that I helped you study to get, by the way, to push this juvenile arrangement. What's changed?"

"Nothing. I do have your best interest at heart, and you will realize that. Until you do, just remember that I always do and I'm always right...Now, if that's all, I have a busy day ahead."

"Too busy to talk to the woman that you're forcing to marry you? Is that how things will be after the wedding because I don't like it?"

The two times that I've spoken to him, he rushed me off the phone and was very short with me. How could he expect me to be okay with that? I didn't know what happened to my best friend, but this wasn't him.

"Maya, relax. I cannot and will not argue with you about this. Enjoy the next few days, okay." After that, he hung up before I could even respond, and I wanted to do nothing but strangle his fucking neck.

That conversation did absolutely nothing but irritated me further. And on top of that, I was going to have to deal with a moody ass Kai. *Way to go, Maya. You managed to have not one, but two asshole men in your life.*

Knowing that I couldn't leave Kai hanging, especially after what we did earlier. I needed to talk with him and reason with him because I knew that he was pissed. It was written all over his face.

Slowly, I walked into the living room and was surprised when I saw him lying there asleep. We had only been up for a few hours, but I guess this was his way of ignoring me.

Too bad for him, because I wasn't going for it. He promised me something earlier, and I figure now would be the perfect time to get it.

18

K ai

THE FEELING of my shorts being pulled is what made me wake up. I thought I was dreaming for a moment. I opened my eyes before closing them again because I had to be dreaming.

Then I felt Maya's warm and wet mouth on the tip of my dick. I lifted my head and was greeted with the beautiful sight of her on her knees with her mouth slowly getting lower and lower as she took me in.

"Maya," I moaned. She sucked on me hard before lifting her head with a big smile on her face.

"Yes?"

"What are you doing?"

"You said that I could taste you later."

"I did say that, but...not that I'm complaining, but what about Jo—"

"Shh. I don't want to talk about that. Right now, I want to feel you come apart while I suck this beautiful thing."

"You're calling my dick beautiful? I obviously didn't fuck you hard enough." She chuckled in response before taking me into her mouth again. "My God…Maya."

"Mmm," she moaned, the vibrations from her mouth were driving me crazy. The more I watched her as she moved up and down on my dick, the closer I got to coming, but I wasn't ready to come yet.

"Come here, Maya." Her eyes looked at me seductively while she continued to suck on my cock a few more times before stopping and standing up.

"Yes."

"Get a condom," I groaned. I was trying to keep it together before I bent her over and fucked her raw.

"No."

"What?" She untied her robe and revealed her beautiful naked body.

"I'm on the pill, I'm clean, and I trust you." As much as I wanted to, I wondered what that meant for her. She wanted me to fuck her with nothing between us. Did that mean something to her? Did *I* mean something to her?

"What about—"

"I want you, Kai. Don't deny me." I couldn't even if I wanted to. My silence seemed to give her the answer that she was looking for because she slipped her robe off and climbed on top of me.

Leaning in, she brought her lips to mine. The feeling of her mouth on mine with her body pressed against me had me concentrating to let her keep control. She wanted to be in control and for right now, I would let her.

I felt her hand move between us. She grabbed my dick and put it at her entrance before sliding down slowly. I watched her as she sat up, her head flying back, and mouth opening.

"Kai," she moaned.

Wild and fucking beautiful...She fucked me fast and fucking hard. "You're so fucking beautiful, Maya. The way you're taking control and fucking me...you were made just for this, to ride my dick."

"Ahh...Oh my—" She started panting and bouncing harder and harder until she came as she screamed my name.

I'd done it. I let her be in control and while it was so good, I needed more. I had this overwhelming need to possess her.

I held her to me as I sat up. While she was still trying to catch her breath, I lifted her off of me and stood. I pulled her up and walked around to the side of the couch. "Bend over." My voice was husky and commanding.

I kissed on her neck and trailed soft sweet kisses down her back. Then I stood up and slammed into her. I'd been patient. I'd given in to her, but in the brief moment of our bodies being apart, I thought about her being with Jonathan, and it pissed me off.

I wanted to punish her. Punish her for all the years that I'd been in love with her. Punish her for not seeing me. Punish her for agreeing to marry Jonathan. Punish her for not being mine.

"Kai," she hissed and grabbed my thigh.

"Move your hand, Maya." I grabbed both her hands and held them together around her back. Harder and harder, I slammed into her, feeling like I couldn't get deep enough. I needed more.

It was still... "So good...Your pussy feels so fucking good." Her hands that I held started to tremble. I knew that she was close, so I paused and pulled out of her, releasing her arms.

"What are you doing?" She asked.

I laid the blanket on the floor instead of responding. "Lay down. I want to see you when you come." I wanted to see her fall apart, knowing that it was because of me.

She looked nervous as she lowered herself onto the blanket. I didn't waste any time. I was back between her thighs in an instant with her legs thrown over my shoulders.

"Fuck," I groaned. With this angle I was deeper and every single time I pulled almost all the way out before slamming into her and grinding to press against her clit. "How could you?"

"Kai." Her pussy squeezed my cock as she came, soaking me.

"See how wet your pussy is for me? How could you, Maya?...*Fuck*. How could you marry him when your pussy was meant for me, hmm? You can't marry him. He'll never be able to fuck you like I can. Dammit...*Maya*."

I came, emptying every piece of me into her. I'd thought that I was fucking her to punish her. I wanted to look at her, but I think I'd only punished myself. Being intimate with her only made me feel...*more*.

I knew then that I needed to get away for a moment. I wasn't going to be an asshole to her though, so I helped her up and with her robe before grabbing my clothes and heading to the bathroom. I couldn't do this with her if it meant that she was leaving me in the end.

19

Maya

Something had changed in Kai's eyes the moment he came. I'd seen it instantly as if a switch had been flipped. I wasn't sure what exactly had caused the change, only that I knew it had to do with me.

I sat there for a while waiting for him to come back out, but when he did, he was fully dressed. He put his boots and coat on and walked out the front door without saying a word. I'd sat there staring at him like an idiot.

Grabbing my phone off the table, I did what I normally did when I was confused out of my mind...I called Terra. She came over the screen with a smile on her face. "What sexy tea do you have for me this time?"

I shook my head at her. "Seriously, Terra?"

"Sorry. You know I live for this. What's going on?"

"Hell, I don't know. I feel like I've done something

wrong, but I have no idea what that is. Well, that's not necessarily true. Kai and I sort of...had sex."

"Oh, my God. What?"

"I know. We did, and it was...amazing. Then, Jonathan called, and it was a mess after that."

"Because Jonathan called?"

"Because I answered for him and then I sort of needed Kai to leave so I could talk to Jonathan. I could tell Kai was mad, but I wanted to get Jonathan to cancel the wedding, which didn't work. Then, I came back out here, and we had some very rough and hot sex. Afterwards, he just seemed, I don't know, like he didn't want to be near me."

"Sheesh. I can't imagine why."

"Terra."

"Maya, you're a smart woman. What do you think Kai is upset about?" I knew why Kai was upset, but he knew the situation from the beginning.

"I mean, obviously he's upset that I spoke to Jonathan right after we had sex. I know that he feels like we missed our chance, but one minute he was fine and the other he wasn't."

"Maya, if the roles were reversed, if Kai was supposed to marry another woman and it was him spending sexy time with you and then speaking to the woman that he was supposed to marry, how would you feel?"

"Unwanted and used. I would feel like he was using me for sex and like he doesn't care. I would want him to choose me even if it was a hard thing to do."

"Well, there you go. Whether you feel like you don't or not, you have a choice, Maya. I understand you being nervous because you feel like you know Jonathan and think he's serious about taking legal action, but...you still have a choice. I don't care what legal paperwork he's sent you; he's got to be full of shit about at least part of it."

"I don't feel like it. I've seen Jonathan work. He's ruthless and while I never thought he would be that way with me, I also never thought that he would be as firm as he has. He seems serious about this, Terra."

"And you still have a choice. One of those choices is letting Kai go because he could get hurt from this. Scratch the could, he will get hurt from this. He's in love with you, and Jonathan is his best friend. He'll either have to deal with his best friend or watch you marry him. You have a choice, but you need to make it quickly."

I thought about her words long after she had hung up. Kai still hadn't come inside, so it gave me time to think and Terra was absolutely right. I had a choice. I knew the choice that I wanted to make, but was I strong enough to make it?

20

Kai

From where I was sitting, I could see the door open and Maya walking out. It was cold as hell out here, but I couldn't bring myself to fuss over her at the moment. I was done with whatever this was, and it sucked because we could have been something great.

I'd pretty much made it up in my mind this morning that I was going to speak with Jonathan myself. It wasn't like he loved her in that way, so I wouldn't be betraying him.

I knew Jonathan and knew that whatever threats he was using toward Maya was all talk. He'd never get his team of lawyers involved because he would never hurt her like that, but for some reason she believed otherwise.

I was going to talk to her about it. I was going to make her see reason first and tell her that I was going to speak with Jonathan, but before I could, she fucking dismissed me.

Then she'd come to me when she was done and because I can't deny her for shit, I'd give in too quickly. I'd enjoyed every moment of being as close to her as humanly possible. I enjoyed having her body pressed against mine and most of all, I'd enjoyed being inside of her with nothing between us.

Then the moment was over and all I felt was that she was using me. She'd never even paid me any attention before and suddenly, now she did. I couldn't do it. I couldn't be a temporary fix for her when I've wanted her for so long because if she didn't want me, I was going to have to watch her be with him, and I wouldn't do it.

Maya stood there on the porch. First, she looked around until her eyes finally landed on me. Then she stood there, not moving. If she wanted me, she was going to have to take those steps and come to me.

For a few minutes, she just stood there. Then, she turned around and reached for the door, but didn't open it. She turned back around, zipped up her coat, and started walking my way. I took a breath full of relief without even realizing that I was holding my breath because I wanted so badly for her not to walk away.

"Kai...I know that you're upset."

"Do you?"

"Yes, and understandably so."

"Maya, go back inside. It's cold out here."

"I know it's cold, Kai," she snapped at me. "God, you can be so damn irritating and moody."

"Then why even bother with me, Maya?"

"You may as well talk to me because it's not going to work."

"What's not going to work?" I tried to sound as uninterested as possible.

"You being moody. You're doing this on purpose because you want me to get mad and leave so you don't have to talk to me. It's not going to work. I'm staying here until you agree to talk to me."

Silence…I stayed silent until she got mad and kicked a bunch of snow on me. "Stop," I groaned.

"And if I don't?" She kicked a bunch of it on me again and then threw a snowball in my face. In the next second, I was on my feet and running after her and she squealed.

She looked back and was shocked when she saw me right behind her and ended up tripping and falling. I threw snow all over her. I was mad at her, but I couldn't help spending this moment playing with her in the snow.

She grabbed a hold of my coat and pulled me until I fell, and we ended up wrestling in the snow. We played and laughed for a while until she was shivering from how cold she was.

"Come on. Let's get you warmed up, okay? Then I guess we can talk."

21

Maya

KAI WALKED into the living room and started a fire. I grabbed a blanket and snuggled up while Kai went to the kitchen to fix us two cups of hot cocoa. Jesus, I was nervous as hell.

He didn't want to talk to me. I knew that much, but he'd chosen to give me a chance. I felt like this was my one and only time to make the choice. It was either I chose him now or I had to let him go.

"Here you go." He handed me the warm mug. Playing in the snow might have gotten him to talk to me, but I was paying for it by freezing my butt off.

"Thank you." I took my first sip, moaning at how good it was and at the warmth of it. Kai looked at me with lust in his eyes before clearing his throat.

"So, you wanted to talk. What's up?"

"I'm sorry." He looked at me for a minute before turning his head.

"I don't want your apologies, Maya."

"Well, that's too bad because I'm giving it anyway. I know that I've made a mess of things. I shouldn't have slept with you while I was technically supposed to marry Jonathan. All I was thinking was that I couldn't let the opportunity pass to explore more with you. And then...the call this morning."

I winced because I wasn't thinking then, but I see now that it was fucked up to answer the phone. I know if he'd answered it for another woman, I would have been livid, too.

"Yeah. That pissed me off more than anything."

"I get it. I do, but it wasn't what you were thinking. I only wanted to talk to him to try to convince him to drop this fake marriage thing."

"Do you really believe that he would do that to you? I mean, I was pissed at him when he first told me, but honestly, you shoulder some of the blame, too. Why would you even agree to marry him so quickly? From what I can gather, you didn't put up much of a fight."

"Of course, I didn't want to marry him. I expressed that to him, but at the same time, I didn't have a reason to fight it."

"How about your life and freedom? How about marrying someone that you actually have romantic feelings for, Maya?"

"My life isn't as successful as one would think it is, Kai. I'm a thirty-year-old freelance photographer that also has to bartend on occasion if I don't get any good assignments that month. Don't get me wrong, I love what I do, but it's not much. If I were there with Jonathan, well, I could work on my dream. While I do not want to marry him, I was hoping to ask for more time while I was there and work on myself."

"No offense, but that's a stupid reason to sell yourself short." He said dryly, and it pissed me off a little, but more than anything, it made me feel embarrassed.

"What do you know? Perfect Kai that's had everything go well in his life. Sure, you can judge me."

"I damn sure can because your excuse is weak, terribly weak. If that's what you wanted to talk about, if you thought that you would gain sympathy from me...you're wrong."

He moved to stand up, and I panicked because by now I knew that if Kai fully shut down on me, I was screwed. He'd barely wanted to talk to me in the first place.

I reached for him quickly and pulled him back down. "Don't go...please."

"What reason do I have to continue this conversation? You seem to have your mind made up."

"Terra...Terra said that I had a choice, and at first, I didn't want to admit it, but I do. I do have a choice."

"A choice?"

"Yes. I can choose to stop this and do what Jonathan asked or—"

"Or?" His voice held hope even if he didn't mean for it to. He'd put on a good front, but Kai still very much wanted me.

"Or I can choose to try things out with you."

22

Kai

"There is only one flaw to your plan, Maya." I should be offended that there was even a choice to be made. Jonathan could never have her heart. And the way her body called to me...he could never have that either.

"What do you mean?"

"You need to be very careful when making your decision because once you say that you are completely mine...you're done. No more bullshit. No more back and forth. No more changing your mind, Maya."

"Kai—"

"Maya, I'm serious, but before you answer, I would like to know where all of this is coming from."

"Well, I thought about what Terra said, and she's right, I do have a choice. Truth is...I've hidden so much behind Jonathan that I think I've gotten too comfortable...comfortable enough to be tracking my way to him even when he's being unreasonable. I don't want to be comfortable, Kai. I want to be happy."

"And what happens when you have to tell Jonathan about all of this?" I really didn't give a damn, but I wanted to make sure that I had everything taken care of on her end.

"It won't matter." She shrugged. "It won't matter because I'm yours." As soon as the words were out of her mouth, my lips were on hers. I placed my mug down and leaned into her.

"Maya...you don't know what that does to me."

Right there in front of the fireplace, I laid her down and kissed her deeply. We worked to remove each other's clothes and in the next second, I was sliding into her and moving slowly. I wanted her to feel every piece of me.

My only thoughts were of her and how long I've wanted her to be mine. And once we were both satisfied and she came, I followed her with her name on my lips, holding back the three words that I'd wanted to tell her for years.

"Stay here." I kissed her and then went to the couch and grabbed a bigger blanket and a pillow. I went back to Maya, laid down, and pulled her into my arms. For the first time, I could hold her like this, knowing that she belonged to me.

I was happy, and that's all that mattered. Anything else, including Jonathan, would be dealt with later. Right now, it was all about me and the woman in my arms.

"It's too early to sleep," she teased.

"I'm not going to sleep. I just want to hold you for a while." She turned on her side and tilted her head toward me for a kiss.

"This feels nice."

"It does. I never thought we would be here."

"We could have been if you would have told me a long time ago how you felt."

"You're right, but there's nothing that I can do about that now. All that matters is you're here now."

"What about Jonathan? Do you think he will be mad?"

"I don't know, and I don't care. I told you that once you said you were mine, there would be no turning back. I meant that, Maya."

"I know. I won't change my mind."

"Again."

"What?"

"You won't change your mind again. You won't run away from me again. No more back and forth when your guilt gets the better of you. We made a choice to choose each other, and we owe it to ourselves to see where this goes."

Her smile was all the confirmation that I needed, and I was done with that topic. For the next however many days, we were staying in that bubble with just the two of us. When the time comes for us to face the truth, we will do it together.

23

M^{aya}

WE LAID by the fire for a long time. Eventually, we stopped talking, and I just enjoyed laying there in his arms. Then I heard his soft snores as he fell asleep. I couldn't help but laugh.

After a while, I got up and decided to cook something. Since we'd been there, Kai had been making all of the meals, mainly because I'd been hiding. I figured now would be a good time to cook for him while he relaxed, so I put my earbuds in and started my playlist.

My food wasn't chef-worthy like his, but I definitely knew my way around the kitchen. One of my best dishes was salmon, and I'd spotted some in the fridge, took that out, and placed it on the counter.

Then I got started on peeling sweet potatoes and cutting them up. I grabbed everything I needed for dinner and finished prepping, knowing that the salmon should be at room temperature by the time I was done and it was.

I put the food on and started cooking. I was having a good time swaying my hips and dancing to the music as I cooked. Then, I felt an arm wrap around my waist, causing me to jump. I turned around to see Kai with a big smile on his face. "Hi," I said after pausing the music.

"It smells good in here. Are you trying to steal my job?"

"I could never, but I know how to do a little something. Salmon is my specialty."

"I'll be the judge of that." He leaned in and kissed me. "I can't believe I fell asleep."

"You snored too."

"I do not snore."

"Yes, you do. It's a cute little snore too…like a little baby," I teased him. "Go relax. I will let you know when everything is ready."

"What if I want to stay here and watch you?"

"Why would you do that?"

"Because I can't believe you're here with me." He didn't say it, but I could look into his eyes and see it. A part of him was afraid that I would change my mind again, but I wouldn't. All my life I was a good girl, doing what was expected of me. This time I was doing what *I wanted*.

"And I will still be here after you're done relaxing and I'm done cooking." I lifted my head to kiss him again.

"New deal. While you're finishing the food, I will set the table and pour the wine. Once we're done, we can take a shower together because the amount of times I've imagined you in there with me is insane."

"Mmm…If you want to eat, you may want to stop talking."

"Is eating you an option instead?"

"Kai."

"Alright...This dinner seems important to you. Sorry." He said before leaving to go back to the living room.

The dinner was important to me because I wanted to treat him just as nicely as he'd treated me. I wanted to show him that I was interested in *him* and not just for sex.

I felt so guilty when he pointed out how much I'd ignored him. I didn't do it on purpose, but once he pointed it out, I realized that I'd never treated him fairly. I just assumed that everything he'd done was because of Jonathan. I never would have thought that he cared about me and now I wanted to show him that I cared about him, too.

I didn't know how many days we would have here together before we had to first speak to Jonathan and then return home. All I knew was that I planned on spending those days making sure that Kai knew just how much I wanted him.

24

Kai

"Tell me about your family," Maya said. We had just sat down to eat, and I must say, she did, in fact, make an excellent salmon.

"You don't have to, Maya." I knew she felt bad about never asking about my family, but I didn't want her to feel obligated or anything. If she was going to ask, I wanted it to be because she genuinely wanted to know.

"I don't have to, what?" She smiled awkwardly. "I'm not asking you about them because of what you said. I genuinely want to know more about you and your family."

I studied her for a moment but then decided not to worry about it. We can't change the past and that includes how we interacted with each other then. But we can do better right now...and she was trying. That's all that mattered.

"My parents are both lawyers. Which is why everyone was so surprised that I wanted to be a chef, but I've always loved cooking. My folks were busy during the week. Most of the time, I stayed with my nanny during the week, but on weekends...it was our time."

"Interesting. I would have never guessed."

"Yeah," I chuckled. "On weekends, I would wake up with my mom and help her cook brunch. I would always watch her in the kitchen. I started watching cooking shows and trying recipes that I found online. Soon, I was surprising my parents with dinner in the evenings. They were very surprised when they first tasted my food."

"As was I. I would have never guessed that you were a chef, either." She shook her head, and she laughed.

"What did you think I was?" That's something I had been curious about ever since she showed just how shocked she was at my cooking skills.

"I don't know. Something like a...lawyer if I'm being honest."

"Really? Why?" She was the first person who ever said that. Honestly, the only reason that I didn't follow in my parents' footsteps was because I knew that I couldn't be half as good as them. I wanted to make my own way in something and not be compared to my family. Becoming a chef afforded me the opportunity.

"Well, the only other lawyer that I know is Jonathan. To me, you and he act just alike at times. He has some ways about him that he hadn't always had. There are some things that lawyer Jonathan does differently than the boy I knew."

"Hmm...I guess I can see that." Soon after we were done with our meal, but we sat at the table and talked while drinking wine for a while after.

It felt wonderful. It felt natural. Talking to her was so

easy and while I knew that relationships weren't always easy, I'd hoped that it was a perfect start to a foundation for us.

"You know what my first thought was when I walked in here and found you swaying your hips?" I asked her. At this moment, the wine was talking, but every word was true.

"What were you thinking?" She giggled, no doubt feeling the wine, too. I could see just how much it was getting to her as she looked at me with her head slightly down. Her eyes fluttered open and closed. She looked so fucking beautiful.

"How I can't wait to get out of here so I can take you out dancing."

"Why wait? We have an open space right there, and I'm sure you have music on your phone. Come on." She stood up and held out her hand. "Dance with me, Kai."

25

Maya

JUST AS HE'D been happy to see me dancing, I'd been imagining that I was swaying my hips against him. I loved to dance, but aside from going with Terra, I'd never gone dancing with anyone.

When I suggested it, the smile on his face spread so wide. He quickly, but smoothly, stood up and placed his hand in mine. "Do you like John Legend?" He asked.

"Who doesn't like John Legend?" I thought he'd play what most people would in this situation, *All of Me,* but he didn't. The music started to play from the speaker that he quickly hooked his phone up to and *You & I* started to play.

He pulled me in slowly while he looked me directly in the eyes. It was too much, and I looked away. Without pausing, he lifted my head and leaned in to kiss me without stopping.

We danced through half of the song, but when the next chorus part of the song came on, Kai turned me around so that my back was against his chest. He wrapped his arms around me tightly and as we danced, he started to sing.

That was another thing that I learned about Kai. He could sing. I couldn't help but close my eyes as I listened to him sing to me... then the song was over and so was our dance but as we stopped moving, it was only a pause before we were moving again.

Kai once again turned me around, but this time to face him. Then, he moved me back until my ass hit the side of the table we didn't use.

I'd changed before dinner into a dress that stopped quite a bit above the knees. At the time, I thought that it was overkill. I mean, it wasn't like we were going out to a restaurant, but now, as Kai rubbed his hands up my dress, I'm glad I did.

"You have the most beautiful legs," he said as he looked into my eyes. This was something that I knew he loved to do: stare at me while he made me come apart. For me, it was intense and I tried to keep my eyes on him, but failed every time.

"Look at me, baby." His hand kept trailing until it made it *there,* and he groaned. "No panties. You pretend to be a good girl, Maya, but only a bad girl would have on no panties with this short as fuck dress on. You wanted to be fucked on this table, didn't you?"

"Yes." I'd barely made it through dinner as I imagined him fucking me senseless on the table.

"Fuck," he moaned when his finger slid into me. "You're so fucking wet. I have to taste you. Lay back for me."

I did as he asked, laid back and watched him slowly slide my dress up. Then he bent over and licked my pussy.

The feeling of his tongue as he moved it around my pussy, from my opening to my clit had me close to coming in no time.

It was intense and right when I was on the edge, Kai slid what felt like two fingers inside of me and gently rubbed. I came, back arched, my hands in his hair, and it felt fucking amazing. "Kai," I moaned.

"Fuck. You taste good." He kissed his way from my pussy, up my body, and to my lips. His face and beard were full of my juices. Grabbing the back of his neck, I pulled him in and licked from his beard to his lips before kissing him.

Our tongues danced with passion and at times, fought for control. Then he positioned his dick at my entrance and pushed into me, filling me up. I couldn't help but gasp at the feeling. He was painfully hard and while it felt good, it hurt like hell, too.

"Maya," he moaned over and over just as I was moaning his name. His body had been pressed against mine as he moved at a quick pace before slowing down and standing up.

He moved in and out of me slowly as he looked down and watched. "So beautiful...The way your pussy takes my dick is...just...beautiful, baby."

"Kai...please." His thrusts were slow, and it tortured me because it kept me right on the edge. It was like hanging off the edge of a cliff but never falling.

Two hard thrusts and a few slow ones. He did this tortured dance over and over until I couldn't take it anymore. Then, he gave it to me, harder and harder until I came. He continued thrusting as I rode out my orgasm, and then he was falling right over the edge behind me.

"Wow," I panted as I tried to catch my breath. Kai was still in place, trying to do the same. A few minutes later, I winced as he pulled out of me and looked at him with wide eyes.

"What's wrong?"

"No way you're still hard." He chuckled at me, but I was serious.

"Tired?"

"A little, but more importantly, I would like to be able to walk tomorrow...and my shit is sore." He laughed before kissing me softly.

"Come on. You go shower, and I will load the dishwasher."

I made my way to the room, grabbed an oversized shirt, and headed to the shower. A little while later, the shower door opened and Kai stepped in. I looked at him, narrowing my eyes in suspicion.

"No sex," he laughed again. He thought that it was funny, but I could assure him that my vagina did not. She hadn't had anything close to that much action.

"No sex, I promise. We're going to shower and then we'll lay on the chaise lounge and watch a movie. How about that?"

"Sounds good." And it did because as much as I loved the sex, I had to know if it was more to us. Will things be awkward when we take sex out of the equation?

26

Kai

THE BEST THING about tonight was that I got to have all of Maya. In such a short time, we had plenty of sex. We talked some, but I wanted to show her that I've wanted her for more than her body.

So, as promised, I didn't touch her in the shower sexually, only to help her wash her body. Then I washed mine as I watched her, still shocked as fuck that she was finally mine. When we were done, I dried us both off and we headed to the bedroom where I had started the fireplace.

I pulled on a pair of boxers while she put on one of my shirts. Then, I pulled her to the chaise lounge and I sat down before pulling her down to sit between my legs. "What movie do you want to watch?" I asked her.

"Anything will be fine." I gave her the remote and after a couple of minutes, she put it on something. I couldn't focus on the movie list because my mind was too focused on her as she laid in my arms, snuggling close to me.

She pulled up *The Pacifier* and told me that it was one of her favorite movies. I'd seen it before, so it made it easier for me to ignore it and focus on her. Her laughter filling the room was the most beautiful sound to me.

I sat there smiling as I enjoyed every moment and when it was over, I picked her up and walked a few steps to the bed. I hadn't even asked if we were both sleeping in here. I just knew that I wouldn't be leaving her tonight.

"Every night I wished that you were in here with me," she mumbled sleepily.

"I wanted to be," I confessed. "Every part of me wanted to come in here with you, but only when you were ready, and you weren't."

"I would like to think that I was ready, but you're right, I wasn't. I'm ready now, though." She tilted her head to kiss me.

My eyes were getting tired, but I tried my best not to fall asleep as she closed her eyes. For a while, I just wanted to watch her. She looked beautiful as she laid there in my arms, and I swore then that I would never let her go.

The touch of her hand on my cheek was what woke me. I didn't immediately say a word and neither did she. She just stared into my eyes as if she could read my entire soul.

"You're so beautiful," I whispered before leaning in and pecking her lips.

"Sure. Tell me anything." She rolled her eyes.

"I promise. I would never lie to you. You're truly the most beautiful woman that I have ever seen."

"Ugh...Kai, please don't make me climb on top of you and ride you until you come." I couldn't help but laugh. "I'm so serious. I'm trying here since I'm really sore, but I'm this close." She held up her hand to show me her index finger and thumb. "I'm this close to saying forget it."

"Baby, as much as I would love that, I know that your body needs rest so, no sex today. But don't worry. Tomorrow I'm going to spend every waking moment with my dick buried inside of your warm and wet pussy."

"Mmm...That didn't help," she whined, causing me to chuckle.

"Seriously, I'm getting up. You stay right here and rest. When I get done in the bathroom, I will fix breakfast."

"You've been doing most of the cooking. Why don't I do that?"

"Not this time, sweetheart. Rest for me, okay?"

"Alright," she smiled as she laid back down. She looked beautiful, content, and happy...and I was happy knowing that those feelings were all because of me.

27

Maya

EVERY MOMENT that I spent with this man, I wondered how the hell I didn't see him for who he was before. The man that I'd been spending my time with seemed to be everything that I'd wanted in a man and more. How had I not seen that?

Was I really that blind? The way that he's treated me the entire time that we'd been here had made me understand his frustration with me. Hell, I was frustrated with myself.

It was clear that everything that he had done for me had more to do with him as a person and not Jonathan. He'd done those things because he cared, just like he's been taking care of me while we're here.

Hell, even when we were bickering back and forth, he still took care of me, cooking for me and giving the room to me to make me comfortable.

I was just happy that I got a chance to see the real him before it was too late. Oh God, what would I have done if we hadn't gotten stuck out there in the snow?

What would have happened if we had gotten cleared out the next day or if we hadn't been snowed in long enough for us to work through our issues?

Would I have found the nerve to tell Jonathan no? Would I have found the nerve to tell Kai that I did see him and that I was just afraid to show it? Would he have let me marry Jonathan?

Would he have stood by while we made a life together, never knowing how good we could be together? Would he have still wanted me?

It made me sad to think about it. Though I would have put up a fight to get out of marrying Jonathan, a big part of me knew that it wouldn't have been a huge one. I would have married Jonathan and regretted it my whole life, all because I couldn't see what was right in front of me the whole time.

I wouldn't worry about that now, though. I was happy and no matter what, I would hold on to that. Plus, my man gave me orders to rest, so I laid back and closed my eyes.

Unfortunately, Kai was only in the bathroom for maybe five minutes when I heard some loud knocking coming from the front door. At first, I thought it was strange because weren't we snowed in? Who could it possibly be?

Then, the events of the previous day had played in my head, and I wasn't sure if Kai had checked the roads again. We'd been so busy caught up in each other that I was sure that neither of us even thought about it. Which meant there was a strong possibility that we could have left yesterday.

Assuming that it was the guy that runs the cabin and not wanting him to see my naked ass, I threw on Kai's boxers under his shirt that I was wearing. I checked in the mirror to make sure that I didn't look too bad. Then I headed for the door, pausing when I got close and saw Jonathan through the glass on the door.

Oh, my God. What the hell was he doing here? I hadn't spoken to him, so he could tell me that he was coming. I didn't have a missed text or anything when I checked my phone earlier. Now he was here. What kind of game was this that Jonathan was playing?

"I can see you there, Maya. Are you going to let me in?" Well, I guess I had no choice. Then, I looked down at my clothes...Kai's shirt and boxers. What was Jonathan going to think?

28

Kai

THE ROOM WAS quiet when I stepped out of the bathroom. I figured that Maya either went to the other bathroom or was in the kitchen fixing some breakfast. Which canceled out my plan to have a taste of her again.

She was sore so I would not fuck her, but I damn sure wanted to have another taste of her sweet pussy.

I dried off and then I remembered that none of my stuff was in this bathroom, so I wrapped my towel around myself and walked out to the other bathroom. I paused when I heard Maya's voice.

At first, I thought that she was on the phone, but then it became clear that we weren't alone. As I got closer to the living room, the person said something and I recognized Jonathan's voice.

What the fuck?

I was too damn shocked and irritated to think about the fact that I didn't have any clothes on. I just knew that when I stepped around the corner Maya looked nervous as she looked at Jonathan. That immediately put me in defense mode, not for me, but for her.

Was I wrong for touching her before speaking to Jonathan? Maybe, but I'm not sorry about it and I wouldn't let him upset her.

Jonathan, noticing me, turned his head and narrowed his eyes before turning them back to Maya. I walked to my suitcase, grabbed some joggers, and slid them on. Then I walked over to them and stood in front of Maya, separating her from him. "Jonathan, what are you doing here?"

"Is that what we're addressing first?"

"Yeah, it is."

"Shouldn't it be the fact that you didn't have on any clothes while my fiancée has on your boxers and shirt?" I slowly turned to Maya, taking a moment to appreciate how much it satisfied me that she was covered in *me*.

I couldn't help the smile that formed on my face, but it faded as my eyes landed on her face. She was so fucking nervous that she was damn near in tears and it made me feel angry and possessive. Without thinking or giving a damn about anyone else, I stepped back and put my arms around her. I pulled her to my side and kissed her forehead.

"It's going to be alright, baby," I whispered to her. For some reason, Jonathan was being an asshole to her all of a sudden, and I was about to get to the bottom of it.

"Kai, what the fuck? Maya?" He groaned, and she flinched.

"Don't...don't address her. This is between you and me. We will discuss it, but you talk to me."

"I'm talking to the woman that I'm supposed to marry."

"*My* woman. You're talking to my woman, and I'm asking you politely for the last time to address me."

"Fine. I'll fucking address you."

"One moment," I said before turning my back to him and speaking to Maya. "Go to the room and relax." Her bottom lip trembled, and it pissed me off because she should have never been in the situation in the first place. "No tears. Go relax because I got this." I kissed her and sent her to the room. Only when I heard the bedroom door close did I turn back to Jonathan.

"So, I ask you to bring my fiancée to me and you fuck her?" I had to work hard to remember that this was my friend that I was talking to, and that I hurt him because when he called her 'fiancée' it made me want to snap.

"I didn't sleep with your fiancée...I claimed what was mine. Now, I admit that I should have spoken to you first. Hell, I even tried to ignore my feelings for her, but I couldn't. I've loved that girl for a long time, and I just couldn't deny us this chance to see what could happen because once she walked down that aisle I was gone. I wasn't going to watch her be happy with someone else. And on top of all of that, I'm still trying to figure out your reasoning for this bullshit anyway, because despite what Maya thinks, this isn't like you."

"You've been in love with Maya? Because this is the first that I'm hearing about it or even see any attraction between the two of you."

"And when was I supposed to show you that? You don't come home. We always visit you, and when Maya, your best friend, needed anything it was me that was there for her. You expect me to always be near her and never feel anything? She's...she's amazing, Jonathan. I've known that, but never made a move because I thought that she had feelings for you."

"No. She didn't. She—"

"Then, why were you trying to force her to marry you? Again, I admit that I should have spoken to you first, and I apologize for that. I don't apologize for loving her, and I can't give her up."

"You wait until a couple of weeks before I'm marrying her to—"

"Was."

"What?"

"Was going to marry her...Past tense. I'm not giving her up."

"No, you're not." He smirked. Smirked...He fucking smirked while I was standing there ready to kill him if he even tried to take Maya away from me.

He flopped down on the couch and took a deep breath. "You two are so fucking irritating and exhausting. My God, the lengths that people have to go through to make you see sense is ridiculous."

"Jonathan, what the hell are you talking about?"

"Did you really think I didn't know that you were all in love with Maya? Damn, man. You talked about her all the fucking time. Every single time that you saw her you would go on about it forever, and when you didn't see her you would call and ask about her. If we were together in a room, your eyes were on her no matter what was going on."

"You knew that I had feelings for Maya?"

"Isn't that what I just said?"

"Then why would you try to marry her?"

"Damn, Kai, can you take some of that pissed-off possessive male shit out of your brain for a minute and use your head? I wasn't going to marry Maya, but I knew that you two would break if I forced you to. It was all fake...The whole trip."

"I drove my ass up here in this snow and she was fucking terrified. Wasn't shit fake about it?"

"Also planned. I checked the weather and knew that it was supposed to get bad around that time. I contacted the cabin rental place earlier in the week and booked it. How do you think it was stocked up with everything that you love to cook with? I told them what to buy." He shrugged his shoulders as if it was no big deal that he had us stuck in a damn winter storm.

"I paid him extra not to dig you guys out for a few days. I figured if you were stuck here, eventually you would confess your feelings toward each other because I see the way that she looks at you, too."

"What if things had gone wrong, Jonathan? The weather changes, roads get closed...Anything could have happened."

"But it didn't." He shrugged.

This time it was me who flopped down on the couch. He had planned the whole thing. "Fuck, Jonathan. Maya was fucking terrified. Couldn't you just, I don't know, invite us out to dinner to do all that?"

"I could have, but I love the dramatics and extra shit. You know that." He laughed.

"Kiss my ass, Jonathan." That only made him laugh harder and as much as I tried not to, I ended up laughing with him. "You're an idiot."

Just as we quieted down, I heard Maya coming down the short hallway and then she was there, fidgeting and looking nervous still. "Come here, baby." I held out my hand to her.

"Everything okay?" She looked between Jonathan and me.

"Yes, baby. Everything is fine other than your friend being an idiot."

"What do you mean?" She asked as she sat between us. He went into his whole spiel of how he planned the whole thing. She didn't relax after learning the truth. Her eyebrows furrowed and her nose wrinkled, and I knew that she was pissed.

"Kai's right. You're a fucking idiot, Jonathan. All of this was for nothing. You seriously could have put us in a damn group chat, and it would have been better than this."

"The fact that you were wearing Kai's clothes tells me that it wouldn't have been. You wouldn't have made the progress you've made at a restaurant or in a group chat."

"Maybe, but we almost didn't give in at all. Had it not been for Terra talking me into not having any regrets, I wouldn't have given in. This was stupid, Jonathan."

"Maya." He sat up and grabbed her hands. I wanted to snatch her away, but again I had to remind myself that they were still best friends, and he never actually wanted her.

"Do you remember the other day when I told you that I was doing what was best for you and that I always have your best interest at heart, that you didn't understand, but one day you would realize that I was right?"

"Yes."

"Today is that day, Maya. I knew that you two would have kept living and passing each other by unless I stepped in. That's my job as both yours and Kai's best friend, to look out for you. I won't be sorry for that."

29

Maya

As much as I wanted to be mad at Jonathan, I couldn't be. I had the most amazing time with Kai. Hell, even when we were arguing back and forth, it made me feel alive.

"Your methods were definitely over the top, but...thank you. I had it in my mind that Kai didn't like me as a person, so I definitely would have never guessed that he had feelings for me."

"He's just a moody asshole."

"He's definitely that." I giggled when Kai looked at me with a sour face. "What? You are moody. You wouldn't even talk to me on the way up here."

"I thought you were marrying this idiot and as I said before, you never saw me, so I was frustrated." That was one thing that still bothered me. I was so blind.

"I see you now." I pulled his head down to me and kissed

his lips before leaning back into his chest. At that moment, I wanted nothing more than to be so close to him that I was damn near in his skin.

"Enough of the mushy shit," Jonathan said. "I'm going to get out of your hair since I clearly interrupted something."

"But, wait. What made you come down, anyway?"

"I was just waiting for the right time. When the roads were cleared yesterday and I didn't hear from you, I knew that something had happened. So, I got up early to drive down and see if what I thought was true. I have to get back, though. I have some work to get done."

"It's always work with you. You should come back with us. We could hang out."

"Nah. This is new. You two need to work things out. I promise I will visit soon."

"How soon?"

"Give me a couple of weeks. Maybe Valentine's day since we have to do our friend's date."

"She's going to be busy," Kai grunted.

"She was my friend before she was your woman," Jonathan teased.

"Or—" I interrupted before Kai could respond. "You could come, and we could go on a double date. I'll hook you up." I winked at him.

"Oh, please. Hook me up with who?"

"Don't worry about it. I have just the person in mind."

"I'm sure you do…I'll think about it, okay?" He said before standing up. Kai and I stood up, too. Jonathan pulled me into a tight hug. "Be happy, Maya. You deserve it." And with that, he was out the door.

I turned around in Kai's arms and looked up at his handsome face, wrapping my arms around his neck. "Still want me now that it's not taboo to have me?" A part of me feared that he wouldn't want me now that things were out in the open. Like, maybe it was the thrill that he was after instead of me.

He lifted me and wrapped my legs around him before leaning in and kissing me. "Let me show you how much I want you," he said before heading to the bedroom.

He laid me on the bed gently. "Don't ever think that I don't want you. I will always want you, Maya." He slowly took off his clothes and as every piece dropped, revealing his body, my desire rose. I wanted nothing more than to taste him.

"Wait." I pushed him back as he started to climb into bed.

"What?" He looked confused.

"I want to—"

"You want to, what? Open your mouth and tell me what you want." I wrapped my hand around his dick and brought my mouth closer to him.

"I want to taste you," I said before slowly taking him into my mouth. His hand immediately went to my head to push me down harder and faster, but I didn't give in. I kept the same slow pace because I knew that it would drive him crazy.

It made me feel good to have this man coming undone with my mouth and hands. Every time I moved up and down or sucked harder, I got more and more turned on. His grunts, groans, and moans were sounds of perfection. And when he couldn't take it anymore and I knew that he was close to coming, nothing was going to stop me from taking him there, not even him.

"Fuck...Maya. I'm going to come if you don't...Oh, fuck." He grunted as he came. I continued sucking his dick until he calmed down, and then I sat back and smiled at him. "I thought I was supposed to show you how much I wanted you."

"You've done plenty of that, even when I was too blind to see it. I figured it was my turn to show you...Now, come lay with me."

While I would love to have sex with him right now, I wanted nothing more than to lie in his arms for a little while. We had a whole day ahead of us, but just for now, I wanted to lie here in this man's arms...*my* man's arms.

∼

We spent two more days at the cabin before heading home. Those two days were something I could have never imagined. We cooked and catered to each other. We watched movies and danced.

We took warm baths together and of course, we would always end up screwing each other's brains out. And even though we knew that we could leave, neither of us wanted to. We wanted to stay right there for a little while longer with only each other around.

Now, we were on the road headed back home and I couldn't help but think about our road trip coming here. It was crazy how fast things could change.

"What are you thinking about over there?" Kai asked suddenly.

"How moody you were on the way up there." We both laughed.

"I was so fucking angry...at you and Jonathan."

"Yeah, you were pretty mad, and the gas station stop. Shit, I was scared to say something to you. You were pacing back and forth, yelling at your phone. I'd never seen you like that before."

"And you probably won't again unless it's over you because that's why I was so pissed then. You were scared out of your mind, and Jonathan was acting like it was no big deal. I really wanted to kick his ass."

I couldn't help but laugh. Jonathan was crazy and this whole thing was silly. He really did go to the extreme just to show us that he knew that we both had feelings for each other. He's an idiot.

After a few minutes, we fell into a silence, and of course, that was all I needed to fall asleep. It must have been a smooth ride because by the time I woke up, we were pulling up to my place.

"Had a good nap." He teased me. "You got a little slob on your cheek there."

"I do not slob in my sleep."

"Are you sure? You sure as hell slobbed on me last night." Horrified, I gasped. *Did I really slob on him?* "I'm just teasing you. You didn't slob on me." He laughed.

"Asshole." We both laughed, but it ended with a heavy sigh from him. I looked over and saw that he was looking straight ahead. "Hey, what's wrong?"

"I've had a great time with you this week, but—"

"Oh, God. Don't tell me you want to end things." I lowered my head to my hands.

"Fuck no. Maya, look at me...No, I don't want to end things. Why would that be your first thought?"

"I don't know. You said 'but' and but is never good."

"But is just a word, baby, nothing more."

"Okay. Sorry. What were you going to say?" He smiled and shook his head. "Continue."

"I've had a great time with you this week, but as much as I would like to be with or near you every day, kind of to make up for lost time, I want to respect what you want and need. So, what do you want, Maya?"

"I want you, Kai. So, whatever that means for you, that's what I want." His lips curled up in a smile. Then he leaned in and kissed me. I will never get enough of his lips.

"Let's get you inside." I reluctantly left the car and walked to the back to get my bags. "Got it."

"At least you sound nicer than you did when you grabbed my bags when you picked me up. Moody ass."

"Tease me about that one more time, sweetheart, and I'm going to have something to tease you about."

"Like what?"

"Like you begging me. What should it be for? Should it be you begging me to come or you begging me to stop coming?"

"Please do. Do that…I want that, all of that." The look in his eyes let me know that I better be careful, but fuck it, I wanted it.

His only response was a wink, and I wasn't sure what that meant. He didn't say another word, just grabbed my bags and made his way up the steps.

I unlocked the door and thanked God that Terra wasn't there. "Want to stay for a little bit?" *Please say yes.*

"Sure, I'll stay."

30

Maya

"WHAT THE HELL IS GOING ON?" I jumped when I heard Terra's voice. I knew that she would be home by now because it was late, but I was hoping she wasn't.

When we made it inside, Kai and I decided to order lunch. We ate, talked, and of course, took things back to the room. After some very good sex, I still wasn't ready for him to leave, so he stayed.

Then he fell asleep, and I didn't wake him up. I knew that it was new, and that's why I want him to be literally right there at all times, but it felt so good to be with him. I finally woke him up, but only because I knew that he had something to do early in the morning.

"Maya...You have definitely left out some details. I haven't heard from you, so imagine my surprise when I come home, and Kai's car is parked out front. What the hell happened up there?"

"A lot. A lot happened."

"Well, you're gonna have to be more specific than that. You left here engaged to Jonathan who happened to be your best friend and you're now, what, with Kai who is also Jonathan's best friend?"

"Basically, yeah."

"Girl, what the hell?"

"I know, I know. It's a lot. Look, I took your advice and decided to explore things with Kai and, Terra, they were more than amazing. He was so loving and caring. Even when he was still mad at me, he took care of me. Then when he made that confession, I was floored."

"I remember." She folded her arms across her chest. "I need to know the rest."

"Believe it or not, I almost fucked it up. I tried to withdraw again, but he wasn't having it. He told me if I said I was his there would be no going back after that. I looked him in the eyes and told him. Then, we sort of got lost in each other, which is why you haven't heard from me."

"And?"

"And Jonathan showed up."

"He showed up?"

"Isn't that what I just said?"

"Okay, and what happened? You're being stingy with the details."

"Well, I was scared shitless because I didn't want there to be a problem between the two of them. Jonathan seemed pissed off, which I could understand since I answered the door in Kai's boxers and t-shirt while Kai was in the bathroom."

"Damn."

"I know, right? Then, Kai came out and looked pissed to hell and sent me to the room. I don't know what they talked about, but apparently this whole thing was some stupid ass plan by Jonathan because he knew we liked each other."

"Oh, my God. Couldn't he just speak to you all about it like a normal human?"

"That's what I said." We both laughed. I still couldn't believe the crazy lengths that his crazy ass went to.

"So, are you and Kai like together now?"

"Yeah." I smiled, thinking about the man that has literally been driving me crazy. "We are."

"Maya, I'm so happy for you. This is going to be so awesome." She hugged me as if I had done something great.

"Thank you. I think so too. Sorry to cut this short, but I'm fucking exhausted from the week. We'll talk more in the morning."

"Alright get some rest." I started walking toward my room when she yelled, "Wait. I need some details. How was it, being with Kai?"

"I don't kiss and tell." I turned around, winked at her, and continued to my room.

"I wasn't talking about the kissing." She yelled.

31

Kai

IT HAS BEEN a week since Maya and I have been back. We'd seen each other just about every day. It was probably unhealthy how addicted I was to her, but I couldn't help it. I just couldn't get enough.

Speaking of her, my phone rang, and I knew from the ringtone that it was Maya. "Hey," I said as I answered the phone.

"Morning."

"It's afternoon."

"Well, it's morning for me."

"Are you just now waking up?"

"Don't judge me when you were the one that wore me out. I was exhausted and needed extra sleep."

"I'm not judging you at all. What's up?"

"I'm obsessing over what to wear. You have to tell me."

Tonight was officially our first date since everything that we'd done was either at the cabin or her place. She asked about what to wear a thousand times, but my answer was always the same.

"I told you to wear whatever you want, Maya. You will stand out in anything."

"You're just saying that, Kai. Please tell me what to wear."

"Stop stressing about it. I'm serious. Just wear whatever you want. It's a very laid-back date. Nothing too fancy for today."

"Ugh," she groaned. "Alright, fine. I will see you at seven," she said before hanging up.

She was really stressed out for nothing. We were going to a movie and then back to my place for dinner. I wanted to keep it simple this time, so that there was no pressure on her, but clearly I was wrong.

"Kai." I looked up to see Karrie, one of three of my employees. "We have everything ready for you."

"Cool. I will be there in a minute."

I had about five more hours of work left before I rushed home to get ready for my date. Hopefully, everything would go through smoothly, but oftentimes in my line of business, clients made last-minute changes that threw me off.

After being a chef at a full-time restaurant downtown for years, I decided to go out on my own, but not for a restaurant. I found clients, most either wealthy or too busy to cook, that needed weekly meals prepared for their families.

So, that's what I did a few days out of the week—stood at a stove all day long and prepared meals. It took a lot sometimes, but it definitely paid well.

I walked into the kitchen of the little place that I worked out of and got started on the shit ton of meals for the week.

"Boss, you really need to learn how to turn down clients. We're at our max," Lauri said.

"I don't hear you complaining when your check increases for every new client that gets started."

"And you never will." She laughed.

It was a long rest of the day, but thankfully everything went through without a hitch. We cleaned up and then it was time for me to head home to meet my woman.

"You girls remember what to do, right?"

"Yes. Go by your house at ten." Karrie laughed when my eyes snapped to her. "Just kidding. Have a sense of humor. We go by your house at nine and make sure everything is hot, fresh, and plated. We set everything up and text you once we leave. We got it."

"Good. Thank you both for helping me out."

"Well, the extra money really helped us say yes," Lauri teased.

"We would have done it for free," Karrie said.

"Thanks, Karrie. Lauri, not so much." We laughed. "See y'all next week."

32

Maya

"You had me worried for nothing. It's been very relaxing." I smiled at Kai as we left the movie theater.

"I didn't have you worried for nothing. You worried yourself. I told you it wasn't that serious."

"It was serious. It's our first official date."

"I don't mean it like that, but I know that we're still getting to know each other more deeply, so I wanted the date to be more relaxing. I didn't want you to be under any pressure."

"You know, if you keep on being sweet to me, I'm gonna start thinking that Moody Kai is an act," I teased. He hadn't been that moody since we'd been back which led me to believe that him thinking I wanted Jonathan was the whole cause of his moodiness.

"Or—"

"Or what?"

"Or you just make me happy." He leaned over and kissed me as we had just made it to the red light.

"Where are we going?" I asked when he passed my exit. Honestly, I didn't care where we were going. I was just trying to brush over Kai's statement. While I'm happy that I made him happy, I was still so scared to fully let go. Could this really work between us after all that time?

Truth was, I was starting to fall for Kai and was scared out of my mind because it was fast. I'd expressed this to Terra before our date and she insisted that mine and Kai's situation was different. She said that it was easier to fall in love with someone that you've known and been around since you were a teenager.

"Back to my place for dinner."

"Did you order in?"

"Hell no. Why would I do that? I prepped everything before leaving home." Just as he said that we turned into a driveway. I was too busy looking at him to see where we were, but the house was beautiful.

It wasn't something you would think a single man would live in. It wasn't humongous but wasn't small either. It looked like something a family would live in and for a slight moment, I could picture us here together with a family.

"What are you smiling at?" he asked me, breaking me from my thoughts. I hadn't even realized that he had gotten out of the car.

"Nothing. Your home is beautiful."

"Thank you." He grabbed my hand. "Let's head inside.

When he opened the door, I expected to sit around and relax while he finished dinner, but I underestimated Kai because that's definitely not what I got.

He stepped back and let me walk in first. There were

rose petals leading from the door all the way to the dining room table where a candlelit dinner was laid out perfectly.

"How did you do this?" I asked as I turned around to face him.

"I have my ways." At that moment, I wanted nothing more than to be in his arms. I wrapped my arms around his neck and kissed him. I don't know how long we stood there and kissed, but it was hard to break away from him.

Afterward, I just stared into his eyes for a moment. I still couldn't believe that this man was mine and oh, how much I looked forward to being with him. I didn't care what happened along the way, as long as we were together.

I could feel it, this was it...and because I knew it, I couldn't help what came out of my mouth. I could no longer hold it in. "I'm falling in love with you, Kai."

"And I'm going to love you always, Maya."

EPILOGUE

Kai
4 years later

JUST LIKE ANY other Saturday morning, I was in the kitchen cooking my wife breakfast. This had become a regular thing since the day we left the cabin the first time. Even when we didn't live together and the times we didn't wake up together, I would still make my way over to her place to fix her breakfast.

I got up and made her favorite omelet with breakfast potatoes, bacon, and pancakes, and the pot of coffee was freshly brewed. I loaded the oversized tray with everything and headed for the living room where we would usually talk about our week or watch cartoons with MaKaila. MaKaila... our baby girl that just turned three.

Things moved pretty fast when it came to me and Maya. I'd waited long enough just to be with her, and I wasn't going to wait much longer. I still remember every detail of the day that I proposed. We'd gone back to Snow Valley for Valentine's and that's where I proposed.

I wanted to do a grand proposal, but that wasn't Maya. Maya liked things simple and meaningful, so I'd thrown out the idea of us going back to Snow Valley because I knew what it meant to her. We were sitting by the fire, getting lost in each other with kisses and touches. She was all smiles and full of happiness.

"You're beautiful, you know that?" I whispered as I looked at her smiling face, feeling like my chest would burst open from the love I was feeling. Her response to me was a giggle. I lifted my hand and rubbed her cheek. "Maya?"

"Yes?"

"Marry Me."

"What?" Her eyes widened as I moved to kneel.

"Will you marry me? I know it's sudden, but nothing would make me happier than to have you as my wife." She rushed into my arms and tears formed in her eyes as she nodded her head over and over.

I gave her a month after the proposal and that was all I was willing to wait. We got married with about 50 of our close family and friends. Nine months later, MaKaila came into this world with her mother's good looks and my attitude...or at least that's what Maya says.

This morning it was just Maya and me. MaKaila was spending her first weekend with my parents. They came to see her often and spent a lot of time with her, oftentimes staying for days at a time, but they lived a little over two hours away, so we needed to be ready.

"Baby?" I said as I came around the corner with the tray of food, seeing her balled up in the corner of the couch. She turned her head to me and I could see her tearing up.

"What's wrong, Sweetheart?" I sat the tray down and moved to comfort her.

"My baby's all grown up." She sniffed. "She doesn't need me anymore."

"Of course she does."

"Kai, you should have heard her. 'I go with Nana and PawPaw, Mommy, You not coming.' I said, you don't need Mommy to go with you. She literally smacked her little mouth and threw up her hands. 'Course not, Mommy. I stay with Nana three days cause Nana say I could." She mocked our daughter, and it took everything in me to try not to laugh, but I failed. "You're not supposed to laugh. You're supposed to make me feel better."

"I am going to make you feel better."

"Oh yeah? How will you do that?"

"Well, first I'm going to feed you. After that, I'm going to lay you down and massage this beautiful body of yours. Then, I'm going to taste that sweet treasure between your thighs…and last but definitely not least, I'm going to fuck you until I give you another baby to cry about."

"Mmm…All of that sounds good, but I don't think it's possible to complete your whole list. You can't get me pregnant."

"Need I remind you of how quickly I knocked you up after you stopped taking birth control?"

"I'm aware."

"Mhm. So, you're challenging me, Wife?"

"Not a challenge, but you can't knock someone up who's already pregnant." She smiled as I gasped.

"I fucking knew it. I told you." I squeezed her tight. "I love you. I love you so much."

"And I love you."

AFTERWORD

Did you enjoy Snow Valley? Are you even a little bit curious about Jonathan and how things will go when Maya sets him up?

Follow me on Facebook and join my group, MJ Mango's Heartache Haven. Soon, you will be able to read that and other short stories via a subscription service. Until then, check out my other stories.

Unexpected Love Series
 Unleash Me
 Unravel Me
 Unbreak Me

The Undying Love Series
 Fighting Love
 Chasing Love

The Wagners

Meant to Be

<u>Love Me</u>
Love Me, Not Destroy Me

ACKNOWLEDGMENTS

Thank you so much to Crystal Johnson Kaiser and team for helping me push this through. The holidays are rough for me after losing my grandmother and I always fall deep.

Coming out, I contacted her and told her that I wanted to release this book on my grandmother's birthday. We had less than two weeks. Her response "we will make that happen for you" and they did. I cannot thank them enough.

Thank you, Ariyana, my mini whom I call my junior pa. Thanks for all the Dr Pepper and Dorito runs while I sat at the computer for hours at a time.

Made in the USA
Columbia, SC
18 June 2025